MYSTRAL MURDER

LEE HANSON
MYSTRAL MURDER

ROOK
RB
BOOKS

MYSTRAL MURDER
Copyright © 2012 Lee Hanson

Published by Lee Hanson as ROOK BOOKS
The Third of **The Julie O'Hara Mystery Series**
First Printed Edition, August 2012

ISBN: 978-09881912-5-9
Library of Congress Cataloging-in-Publication Data

Cover Design by Eli Blyden | www.CrunchTimeGraphics.ncom

For Madi and Syd,
who are as bright and brave as Julie.

MONDAY

1

The questioner stood, a broad-brimmed straw hat casting a shadow across her face. She was very thin and tan, a stylish woman in her forties wearing a slim, white linen sun-dress, perfect for a cruise. "Julie, as a body language expert, do you sometimes find out things you really don't want to know? Like secrets about friends or relatives?"

Everyone in the packed seminar looked expectantly at Julie O'Hara, who was seated on a stool in front of a large screen depicting a series of classic facial expressions. She glanced at her boyfriend, Joe Garrett, a private detective, who was accompanying her on this business/pleasure trip to the Caribbean. He was sipping on a Coke at a table a few rows back in the large

Odyssey cocktail lounge, a venue Julie had chosen over the ship's gigantic theatre. A smile played over his face as he watched her squirm, knowing that she wished he wasn't there.

"That's a very interesting question. Unfortunately the answer is yes. But, fortunately, most of them aren't holding out on me."

A ripple of laughter ran through her audience, including Joe.

"Seriously, though, most of you are probably quite good at spotting deception in people you know. Let's say a man is lying to his wife about something. Very often he'll give himself away verbally. It's hard to miss it when he hesitates before he answers the question, "Where were you last night?""

More laughter…

"And then, of course, when he starts giving you a whole lot of irrelevant information, he's a dead duck."

Every woman in the room was laughing out loud now.

"Okay, so a savvy philanderer might know better than to do any of those things," Julie said, laughing. "But he'd still have a hard time fooling his wife. On a subconscious level, we're all wired to notice signals in each other's body language. Especially faces," she said, indicating the screen behind her.

She rose and walked a couple steps closer to her audience, her hands open.

"Truly, it's a skill anyone can improve if they

know what to look for. In the case of our hypothetical straying husband, his wife might pay particular attention to his *eyes*. A liar tends to blink more often and his pupils may be dilated, too. And those are just a few of the 'tells' our men can't control, Ladies. I hope you'll buy my book and learn the rest. We need to stay one step ahead of these guys."

Everyone was laughing again; it was a good time to wind things up.

"I had a great time today. I hope you did, too. Thanks for coming!"

Julie made her way through the applause to the book-signing table set up just outside of the lounge, stopping to shake a hand here and there. One old gentleman took her hand in both of his and said, "Did anyone ever tell you that you look like Julia Roberts?" The man's wife shot him a look you didn't need to be an expert to interpret.

"Yes, thank you," she said for the umpteenth time. She smiled at both of them and quickly moved along out of the lounge. Joe was already out there unpacking some additional books. He smiled at her and winked his approval.

I may not be Julia Roberts, but I'm a hell of an actress. Who ever thought I'd be doing this?

Writing *Clues, A Body Language Guide* had seemed like a logical next-step in her career, but Julie had never thought past the writing part, never thought of all the publicity and marketing involved in publishing. She had underestimated both the demands on her time and the loss of privacy.

Did I want the book to be a success? Yes, of course.

Did I want a guest spot on The View? NO.

She and Joe were aboard Holiday Cruise Lines' Mystral on a seven-day trip to St. Thomas, St. Maarten and back again, courtesy of her publisher. They had departed three days ago from Port Canaveral in Central Florida, just an hour from Orlando where the two of them lived and worked. The experience *was* exciting, she had to admit.

At the dock, the immense white ship had looked like a sixteen-story building several blocks long, truly an awesome sight. Since both of them were first-time cruisers, there was no denying the thrill they'd felt upon boarding. They had joked about being short-changed on what HCL considered 'Day 1', since the Mystral had set sail at exactly four-thirty in the afternoon on Saturday, when most of the day was gone. They would return to the same port the following Saturday, at six in the morning.

Yesterday, Sunday, the ship had stopped at Parrot Cay, a small island owned by HCL. It was a pure vacation day for Julie and Joe, who had gone ashore, enjoyed the ship's Caribbean Barbeque and spent the afternoon sunning and swimming.

But now, on Day 3, Julie felt like her vacation was over. She had just completed the *Clues* seminar, which was her first scheduled event. Later in the week, she had an open interview with Conde Nast Traveler magazine. Book signings were *de rigueur*, and Julie had to step out of her comfort zone each time to deal with her new, larger audience.

Corporate consultant, trainer, author…none of those hats seemed to fit well.

In the last few years, Julie's focus had changed dramatically. Using her skills in a more meaningful way had become paramount. For example, if not for this cruise, she'd be in Orlando helping select a jury. The defendant had shot a stranger coming through her window in the dark…a stranger who turned out to be her abusive ex-boyfriend. In Julie's opinion, the woman's body language confirmed that she was telling the truth, that she had no idea it was him when she pulled the trigger.

The guy's family, a rough bunch, didn't agree and were calling it murder.

Long story short, Joe was happy to have her safely signing books.

Julie sighed in frustration.

What's so safe about a floating skyscraper?

2

～

Cathy Byrne stepped into the Penthouse Suite and took off her broad-brimmed straw hat, setting it on the top shelf of an entry-way closet full of empty luggage. She could see that her husband, Gill, was on his way out. He was dressed for the warm summer weather in khaki shorts, a golf shirt and topsiders. *No doubt hoping to leave before I got back*, she thought.

What was it about men that they looked better as they got older? Of course, at six-four and broad-shouldered, Gill had always looked good. But now, at fifty-five with that thick silver hair and a perpetual tan, he was striking. He never gained weight, never had to diet. Lines only gave his face more character. *It's not fair*, Cathy thought.

"Where are you headed?"

"Oh, out and about," Gill said. "Captain Collier invited me up to the bridge. How was the seminar?"

"It was very interesting. You should've gone."

"Last night wiped me out; I never expected that game to go so long. I just got up an hour ago," he said, rummaging around on the granite bar looking for his card key.

"It's on the coffee table."

"Oh, thanks," he said grabbing it, heading for the door. He stopped and gave her a peck on the cheek. "See you later. I'll be back in time to get dressed for the Captain's Table."

Just like him to forget about me and do whatever he feels like.

Gill Byrne was a charmer who was used to doing whatever he wanted to do, whenever he wanted to do it. Five years ago, he sold his highly successful national beer distributorship to a global beverage wholesaler for millions. A smart investor, he had doubled his net worth since then and was currently buying every available building in Downtown Orlando.

Gill had acquired wives along with wealth. He married the first one at the tender age of twenty-five; she was only eighteen. Childless, they parted company five years later. The second time around was a shotgun wedding that ended when his daughter, Deidre, was eight. Gill never missed wife number two, but he'd spent the last several years trying to buy his daughter's affection. Not so much because he loved her, but mostly because he had a compulsion to charm everybody. As a result, Dede Byrne was spoiled rotten.

Cathy Byrne was wife number three.

At forty-eight, she took pride in looking several years younger. Turning, she caught her slim image in the mirror on the door. She turned sideways to look even slimmer. The white linen dress looked good with her tan, she thought, sucking in her stomach. *I could stand to lose a few more pounds, though.* She smiled and turned away, looking out the open glass door to the sea.

The large Penthouse Suite where she and Gill were staying was on Deck 10. It was tastefully decorated in soft gray and pale blue, and had a wall of glass with triple sliding-glass doors. The view was simply unparalleled. Adrienne Paradis, Cathy's friend and travel agent, knew that they wouldn't settle for less. And why should they? This was their fifteenth cruise with Holiday Cruise Lines; they were members of the privileged Captain's Club.

Cathy grabbed a Diet Coke out of the refrigerator under the bar and headed for the double balcony. She stood out at the railing, enjoying the warm breeze and the salty air. She really didn't have a care in the world. Except for one thing…

Cathy Byrne was wife number three.

3

Julie and Joe considered themselves lucky to be on Deck 10, although their ocean-view mini-suite was the smallest of the lot. It had navy blue wall-to-wall and a wide-open sliding glass balcony door. Snow white drapes, drawn back on either side, puffed lightly in the breeze. Bleached oak blended with a nautical blue and white striped fabric on the sofa and the bedspread...the large and rumpled bedspread.

"Joe, come in and help me," Julie snapped, smoothing it out. The hard edge in her voice wasn't because Joe was relaxing out on the balcony. And it wasn't about Joe's earlier "slam-bam-thank-you-ma'am" performance, either.

It was about the glass of champagne in his hand.

Julie glanced over at the built-in bar, where the complimentary bottle had sat untouched for two days. *He must have opened it when I was in the shower,* she thought. *I wonder if the coke he was nursing today had booze in it.*

Joe joined AA as a young man, right after graduating from Florida State. She had never seen him with a drink and he had never mentioned any "slip". Julie did a quick calculation: *That's twenty years of sobriety! Shit. We've got to talk about this. But not now, not with the Captain's Table tonight. Don't get confrontational with him now…*

———

Joe had a hard time tearing himself away from the hypnotic view ten decks below. As the Mystral cut her way across the Caribbean, the sea folded and rolled continuously away from the ship's hull in an aqua-blue and white swirl. Having served in the navy and as a recreational diver, Joe was certainly no stranger to boats. But this giant ship was something else. Joe had never been on a cruise ship before, never been on this kind of vacation.

His everyday stresses were gone; he couldn't remember the last time he felt this relaxed. Of course, he knew the feeling was partly due to his having had a "couple" of drinks. So what was wrong with that? He was just a kid when he used to "overdo it". Surely, all these years of abstinence proved that he could stop any time he felt like it. And that was exactly what he planned to do…as soon as the cruise was over.

———

Joe stepped back inside the stateroom and Julie felt the same old tug at her heart. He was so damn handsome in his tux! Tall and tan, with sun-streaked hair and a light beard, the sight of him was almost enough to make her jump back in bed and ask for a redo.

Shaking his head and laughing, he went to help her. "I can't believe you care what the cabin steward thinks. You need to relax, babe."

Like you? Julie thought, her concern front and center again. Instead she just smiled and took a long look at him. *He's not drunk, at least not so anyone else would notice.*

He came around the bed and caught her up in his arms. "C'mon, four thousand people on this ship and *we're* dining with the Captain! And you look gorgeous…" He spun her around so that they were reflected in the mirror over the dresser.

Julie stood in front of him, dressed in a strapless black velvet sheath, her hair in a ponytail tied with a black ribbon. "Four inch heels and I'm still shorter than you," she said, smiling in spite of herself.

"A lot prettier, too," Joe said. "Just one thing, though…for me," and he pulled the ribbon from her hair, allowing the red-brown waves to cascade over her shoulders. "Now, Ms. O'Hara, you're ready for the Captain's Table."

Right. Are you, Joe?

4

T he Mystral's Medical Center had closed for the
day and not a moment too soon, as far as the
medical staff was concerned. With four thousand
passengers and crew, some days in the severely limited
facility were hell. But today, with a virus scare going
around, at least a hundred passengers had either called
or dropped in looking for antibiotics. And they weren't
happy to be told that antibiotics were only effective
against bacterial infections and not viruses.

An independently run operation, the Medical
Center was woefully small and understaffed, primarily
designed to handle ordinary illness and small scale
accidents. Beyond initial diagnosis, the ship's doctors
and staff were capable of stabilizing patients and
providing therapeutic intervention for most things. But
when a patient was seriously ill or injured, it fell to the
chief shipboard physician to make the call whether or
not to evacuate that person to the nearest port hospital.
One such patient had been taken off the ship today and

raised bloody hell about it. "You haven't heard the end of this, Dr. Sinclair! Do you know how much I paid for this cruise?"

Now, with her workday done and another doctor on call, Dr. Michelle Sinclair, the ship's Principal Medical Officer, determined to put that angry man out of her mind.

Breathing deeply, she stood under her shower letting the stress of the day swirl away down the drain. This was her indulgence. Here, in the privacy of her cabin, she ignored the ship's instructions to "limit water usage". Because she didn't need makeup, Michelle's shower usually took up half of the twenty or thirty minutes she spent getting dressed.

She toweled off and used the blow-dryer on her dark, shoulder-length hair. Then she deftly twisted it, still damp, into a smooth knot at the nape of her neck. Choosing clothes took no time at all since officers were required to wear uniforms at all times in public areas. She went to her closet where starched and fitted white shirts were lined up, one after another, with several just-above-the-knee, white straight skirts. Three of the shirts had extra gold braid on the epaulets, for formal occasions like tonight. She pulled out a set and dressed quickly, slipping on a pair of medium-height, white sling-back heels.

She had calmed down and was feeling like herself again when the phone rang. She picked it up with a sigh and, as usual, didn't even get a chance to say hello.

"I know. I'm sorry. Yes, I know that his wife is upset, too. If she was so sure that he's 'going to be fine', she didn't have to get off with him. They aren't traveling alone, after all."

Michelle held the phone away from her ear. When the rant abated she said, "Please don't threaten me. I don't like it," and she hung up. She took a deep breath and calmed herself.

Tonight, once again, she would sit next to Andrew at the Captain's Table.

5

⁓

J ulie and Joe stood outside their stateroom, invitation in hand, looking left and right. When it came to getting around, the elite folks up on the tenth deck still had to navigate the same narrow, labyrinthine corridors as all the other passengers. Thus far, having eaten at the buffet on the Lido Deck, they had never been to the Main Dining Room and they were trying to remember where it was.

Miguel, their cabin steward, spotted them.

"Your stateroom is starboard, right front of the ship. The closest elevator is the one on your right, and your best bet for most areas is to get off at Deck 4. The Main Dining Room is aft, all the way to the rear."

"Of course," Julie said, "thank you, Miguel."

"My pleasure, Ms. O'Hara, Mr. Garrett. Have a nice evening," he said, bowing.

"How to look like a couple of dorks in one easy lesson," Joe said, as they descended in the elevator. Laughing at themselves, they got off on Deck 4.

They barely noticed the movement of the ship as they strolled through the long Photo Gallery and past the Odyssey Lounge, the site of Julie's seminar. Through the windows on their left, the sinking sun splashed pink across the sky and turned the sea to gold. Joe led Julie outside where they simply held hands and admired the glorious sunset for a while.

When they reached the center of the ship, the space opened-up on an area several stories high, with floors of inlaid travertine marble, tall contemporary glass sculptures and palms. Twin winding staircases, their railings agleam with polished brass, led skyward to Deck 5.

Near them on Deck 4, some passengers lined up at the purser's office, while others sipped coffee just beyond them in the Internet Café. On the right, a pianist in a white dinner jacket played Cole Porter on a baby grand piano to the delight of several couples in formal wear who sipped cocktails, smiling and humming.

They stopped to look at a cutaway diagram of the ship's decks.

"Do you want to go through the Casino or the Promenade?" Joe asked. A popular meeting place, the Promenade was up the staircase on Deck 5. It was a giant atrium with boutique shops, casual restaurants and bars.

And that's when Julie made her first mistake of the night with Joe.

"Let's walk through the Casino."

And so they stepped into Circe's realm of gaily flashing machines with their happy siren songs and cascading coins. The slots were all busy, with several machines chanting, *"Wheel-Of-Fortune!"* Blinking lights on top of one drew attention to an ecstatic winner, a middle-aged woman in a fancy gold dress, jumping up and down. Smiling servers dressed in black pants and white shirts with black bowties carried trays of colorful cocktails adorned with fruit.

Joe's pace slowed to a crawl as he avidly scanned every inch of the Casino, his eyes settling on a poker table off to their right.

"Hey, look! It's Gill Byrne. C'mon, let's go say hello."

Joe had done some investigation for Gill Byrne's attorney when Gill divorced his ex-wife. *They had a little girl. That was a big divorce case,* Julie recalled. *And then we went to his wedding.* That was a few years ago and Julie couldn't remember having seen him since then.

"Hey, Gill," Joe said. "How's Lady Luck treating you?"

"See for yourself," Gill said, smiling and pointing to the chips stacked in front of him. "Hi, Merlin," he said to Julie, using a nickname which had become her business moniker. "Cathy said your seminar was terrific."

Oh, my God, that was Cathy who asked that question about family and friends! I didn't recognize her under that big straw hat. And she was so thin! I hope she's okay...

"Yes. I saw her there. Where is she?"

"She's at the cocktail party, getting her picture taken with the Captain. I don't know what for; it's not like they don't take pictures of everybody at the Captain's Table."

"We're sitting at the Captain's Table, too," Joe said, happily. "Honey," he said, turning to Julie, "why don't you go in and join Cathy. You girls can catch up and I'll meet you in the dining room at eight."

Oblivious to Julie's expression, he turned to Gill and plowed right on.

"You guys don't mind if I sit in, do you?"

After a good-old-boys' chorus of "hell, no," Joe pulled out a chair, leaving Julie no choice but to muster a half-smile and walk away...steaming.

Great, just great. Is this how it's going to be all night?

Julie was at a loss; she didn't know how to react to Joe's altered personality. He'd always been so considerate, always put her feelings first. *Maybe I'm spoiled*, she thought. This was Joe's vacation, too, after all. *If he wants to play a little poker, why shouldn't he?*

Because it's not about poker, she told herself, answering her own question. They were on their way to a formal dinner...together.

She was halfway to the Windward Lounge before she got a handle on her negative thoughts. *I'm not going to dwell on that, and I'm not going to worry about the rest of the night, either. Being invited to dine with the Captain on a ship like this is special. I'll enjoy it and so will Joe. I'll stay "in the moment" and leave tomorrow's problems for tomorrow.*

As a body language expert, Julie knew that smiling was often the first step out of the blues, so she pasted one on and waltzed into the cocktail hour.

6

There was nowhere left to sit in the Windward Lounge, as passengers with Second Seating in the Main Dining Room were all gathered there waiting for their turn to be photographed in their finery with the Captain and two officers. The early birds sat chatting on comfortable sofas and club chairs, while the late arrivals mingled on the dance floor. A string quartet played light classical music, a pleasant background which didn't interfere with the hum of conversation.

Julie looked around the room, admiring some of the formal wear. *It's nice to see people dressed so elegantly*, she thought. *The occasion to dress like this is so rare in Orlando.* She spotted a slim woman across the room wearing a stunning emerald green strapless gown. It was Cathy Byrne. She was talking to two women, both in black. One was a tall, nice-looking woman with salt and pepper gray hair. She was wearing a tasteful knee-length dress with a short tuxedo jacket. The other was a younger, familiar woman in a mid-thigh, lacy number that fit as only a designer original can do. The petite woman, with her clipped pixie hairdo and big brown eyes, reminded Julie of Audrey Hepburn playing *Sabrina*.

Cathy saw Julie and waved her over. "Julie, you look absolutely fabulous!"

"Thank you. So do *you*," Julie said, following her lead.

Turning toward the two women Cathy said, "This is Adrienne Paradis and Lottie Pelletier. We were just talking about how much we enjoyed your seminar."

"Thank you so much. It's a pleasure to meet you. *'Adrienne, of Paradis Travel,'* Julie said, recognizing the younger woman. "Of course! I knew you looked familiar. I've seen your wonderful ads. So tempting! Your office is in Winter Park, isn't it?"

"Yes, for Central Florida. We have quite a few locations in the state."

"More like all over the world," Cathy said.

There was some kind of undercurrent between Cathy and Adrienne that Julie couldn't quite put her finger on. *Were they friends or, what was that new term? Frenemies.*

"Is that right?"

"Yes, it is," Adrienne said. "We've been very fortunate. My parents started the business many years ago in Paris."

"Paris," Julie said wistfully, "that's a city I'd love to visit. My friend and I have been talking about it, in fact."

"Where *is* Joe? Cathy asked, looking around the room.

"I'm afraid he's with your husband," Julie said. "They're aiding and abetting each other in the Casino."

All four women smiled knowingly.

"I must go," Lottie Pelletier said. "I enjoyed your seminar, Julie. Have a good evening everyone," she said, as she followed the Captain and his entourage from the room.

Julie and Cathy arrived in time to join Joe and Gill, who were part of a crowd moving slowly into the Main Dining Room. Joe flashed a big smile at Julie and she returned it, her earlier pique somewhat dissipated. She took his hand and they all moved forward, couple by couple. Looking up at Joe, Julie came to a conclusion despite her concern about his drinking. *So far, it just seems to make him more sociable.*

They were taken aback by the sheer size and splendor of the dining room. Marble columns supported second and third level balconies on either side, each of which accommodated almost as many tables as the main floor. A deep crimson and blue carpet of oriental style covered the whole, wall to wall, and every chair was upholstered in pale blue damask. Snow white table linen drew one's eye to the Mystral's distinctive blue and gold charger plates, set among more polished glass and silverware than the average person could possibly use in a single meal. Sparkling crystal hung like diamonds from recessed tray ceilings, creating a soft glow over each separate dining area.

Julie looked up in awe at a massive chandelier that was suspended high in the center of the room. Ahead of them and directly beneath it was a circular table for twelve. Three ship's officers in their white uniforms - two men and a woman - stood behind their chairs on the far side, smiling and awaiting their guests. Julie recognized Captain Collier as the tall one in the middle. He was tanned and fit, with dark hair going gray at the temples and a trim mustache and beard.

He wears the commander's mantle well.

Although she hadn't met Andrew Collier, she knew quite a bit about him, having looked him up while in the ship's Internet Café. The article said he was "fifty-five, a superb raconteur, having travelled all over the world, and one of the most personable cruise ship captains plying the seas for IICL."

That was nice, but recent news of a smaller ship running aground and tipping over in the Mediterranean was fresh in Julie's mind. She was relieved to note that Captain Collier also had "extensive maritime training and many years of experience"…especially since he was in charge of this floating city she was presently visiting instead of Paris.

"How do you do, Ms. O'Hara?" he said, extending his hand. "It's a pleasure to have you aboard."

"I couldn't be better, Captain Collier. Thank you for inviting us."

He immediately turned to Joe and shook his hand as well. "Mr. Garrett, I believe? Welcome aboard. Are you enjoying your cruise?"

"You bet I am!" Joe said, a little loud. "This is some ship. How many tons is she?"

"One hundred-sixty-thousand, Joe, and she's longer than the Eiffel Tower."

"Wow!"

"Indeed," the Captain said, smiling. He turned toward the Byrnes and their friends. "Hello, Gill, Cathy. Good evening, Adrienne, Dale. It's nice to see you again. Please, have a seat, all of you. Make yourselves comfortable while I welcome our other guests." With that, he quickly moved around the table to greet an older couple on the other side.

Place cards were set all around and they took their seats. Joe and Julie, then Cathy and Gill were to the Captain's right after a ship's officer. To his left, after the female officer, the Captain had placed the older couple and beyond them Adrienne and Dale. Directly across from the Captain sat Jonathan Reece, the writer from Conde Nast Traveler magazine. He was young, black and British. Julie smiled, acknowledging him, and he sketched a little wave at her and Joe.

Waiters with short, pale blue jackets began to pour either a fine Cabernet or Chardonnay for each diner. So unobtrusive was the service that dinner rolls, hot from the oven, and artfully done appetizers seemed to appear like magic: bacon-wrapped scallops with thin sliced salmon and caviar, bruschetta with feta cheese and fresh basil, colorful crudité with dip.

Cathy whispered, "Those folks are celebrating a special occasion," nodding toward the older couple chatting with the Captain and the female officer. "They were chosen at random. He seats them close. I think he wants to make sure they're included in the conversation. Such a wonderful host."

So I've read, Julie thought.

Apparently Adrienne and her strapping, sandy-haired companion knew the seating drill, too. They had immediately found their seats. Now, leaning across the table, she said, "Julie, Joe, I'd like you to meet my husband, Dale."

"Dale Simpson," Joe said, wide-eyed. "Of the Tampa Bay Rays!"

"Hi, nice to meet you. Yeah, that's me. I retired a while ago, though. I work with Adrienne at the agency."

"Nice to meet you," Julie said, thinking, *how long ago could it have been? He doesn't look more than thirty. Certainly younger than her. You'd think she would have used his last name. She diminished him and his baseball career. He's Mr. Paradis now.*

"Hey, great to meet you, man," Joe said. "I'm a Floridian, born and bred. The Rays are my team! I was so damn excited when ya'll won the pennant in 2008. Think they're going to do it this year?"

Ya'll? What alter-ego was Joe slipping into? He sounded like an awestruck southern college kid who'd never been out of Florida. And then it dawned on Julie that the last time Joe had a drink, that's who he was.

Joe and Dale did their baseball-bonding for a few minutes until Captain Collier tapped his glass.

"Well, good evening everyone and welcome. I'm so glad to have all of you as my guests tonight. May I introduce our officers? I'm sure most of you know Dr. Michelle Sinclair, our Principal Medical Officer."

The tall woman in the white dress uniform seated to his left smiled and said, "Good evening," to everyone around the table. She was naturally beautiful, with a light olive complexion and the kind of teeth movie stars pay for.

Forty, perhaps, thought Julie, noticing a few strands of silver in her hair and some laugh-lines about her hazel eyes.

The Captain continued his introductions. "And on my right, this is our Ship's Hotel Manager, Bob Sanchez. He's the fellow behind the scenes who takes care of the cabins, the public rooms and our dining room service, too. That's a big job and no one could do it better."

The somewhat portly officer had a ring of brown hair and a bald pate. He smiled and said, "Welcome aboard, everyone. If you ever need any assistance, please give me a call."

He blushed. Shy? Not likely, Julie thought. This guy might look like Friar Tuck in a white uniform, but he's the boss in his domain. The flush is more likely due to his weight.

"Next to Dr. Sinclair, may I present Phil and Alice Kent, who are celebrating their *fiftieth* anniversary," the Captain said, leading a round of applause.

"A toast," he said, raising his glass, everyone following suit. "To Alice and Phil, may tonight be full of happiness and laughter, and all your tomorrows happy ever after."

The Kents smiled and thanked everyone.

Julie was smiling and thinking, *nice couple, Northerners,* when Captain Collier suddenly turned the spotlight on her. "I'm sure you know our body language expert, Julie O'Hara, and the gentleman at her side is Joe Garrett. Did any of you attend Ms. O'Hara's fascinating seminar?"

Cathy and Adrienne both said they did, and how much they'd enjoyed it. Then Alice Kent chimed in.

"Oh, Ms. O'Hara, I'm such a fan! I saw you on The View. Phil and I loved your seminar and we bought *Clues*, but we forgot to get you to sign it." With that, she pulled the book out of her purse. "I hope you don't mind; I brought it with me." She looked across the broad table laden with food and china and, embarrassed, quickly tucked the book back in her bag. "Perhaps after dinner?"

"Of course," Julie said, thinking, *I love this woman.* "Did you bring a pen?"

"Oh, yes," she said, extracting the pen and waving it.

Adrienne laughed and said, "I wish I'd brought my copy!"

"Me, too," Cathy said. "We'll have to catch you tomorrow, Julie."

"Ms. O'Hara has an open interview later this week," the Captain said. "But I'll let Mr. Reece, from Conde Nast Traveler magazine tell you more about that," and he turned the conversation over to him.

"Uh, hello, everyone. I'm Jon. Like the Captain said, I'm a writer from Conde Nast. I'm here doing a story on cruising, and I'll be interviewing some of the officers and entertainers. Julie's interview is Thursday and we're looking for some audience feedback, so it's going to be in the Odyssey Lounge again. Speaking of that, I'd like to do some passenger interviews, too." Looking at the Kents, he asked, "Would you folks be interested in doing a quick interview after dinner?"

"Oh, we'd love to!" they said in unison.

Look at those expressions, Julie thought with delight. *Their lips are curled all the way up on the sides and they're all teeth. So happy, so genuine. They can't believe their good luck.*

"Excellent," the Captain said. "I think that's a fine idea. And now, may I introduce my good friends, Gill and Cathy Byrne, who are members of HCL's Captain's Club and are enjoying their fifteenth Holiday cruise.

"And last, but certainly not least, I'd like to introduce our good friend, Adrienne Paradis, travel agent extraordinaire, and her husband, Dale Simpson."

"Our" friend, Julie thought, *not "my good friend", not even "my friend."*

Julie's eyes slid over to Michelle Sinclair, sitting on the Captain's left. The doctor was still smiling, but there were subtle changes in her expression. The laugh lines about her eyes that Julie had observed earlier had flattened out. Her beautiful white teeth, upper and lower, were still in view, but her lips, instead of curling up on the outside, were drawn back in an oblong shape.

There's no depth to that smile; she's faking it.

The Captain continued his homage to the travel agent. "Adrienne's prestigious agency, Paradis Travel, is responsible for booking at least four hundred guests on this cruise alone. And we thank you, Madam," he said, raising his glass to her.

"No need to thank me, Captain," Adrienne said, rising. "I enjoy matching people with their perfect vacation, whether it's watching baby sea turtles hatch at night on the Galapagos Islands, or sailing in luxury on a beautiful ship like the Mystral."

Nice pitch. No shrinking violet, our petite friend...

Adrienne raised her glass and said, "Here's to perfect vacations!'

The Captain's table echoed her toast, "To perfect vacations!"

7

Except for the ship's officers and the Kents - who had left with Jon Reece to do their interview - the Captain's dinner guests had gone on to the popular Top Hat nightclub on Deck 12, also in the rear of the ship. The dark floor-to-ceiling windows didn't offer much of an ocean view, as the moon was largely obscured by clouds. Still, the band was good and the place was jumping.

As the evening wore on, the musicians had steadily dialed-down the decibels and tempo until the room was half full. A quarter of those folks were slowly swaying on the dance floor. It was one o'clock and the Captain's guests were resting. Gill was drinking scotch and scowling. Joe, his polar opposite, actually got up to sing with the band and then laughed along with everyone else when they took the microphone away from him. Dale and Cathy were passing the time with banal conversation about their dinner.

"There's no way regular guests get a lobster that size," Dale said.

"And it was sweet," Cathy added. "I'm sure it was from New England."

How could you tell? Julie thought. *You just moved it around your plate, along with the rest of your food. You're too thin. You've had your eyelids done and your upper lip. Are you afraid of age, afraid of losing Gill, or both?*

Julie sighed. Cathy's insecurity was screaming at her.

Julie was so tired. Earlier, at the seminar, she had answered Cathy Byrne honestly. She couldn't "turn it off", couldn't stop reading people. And watching this particular group interact with each other was exhausting.

Worse, Joe had been dancing with Adrienne half the night, until she finally got the message that Julie was pissed and left.

"Joe, let's go. It's late."

"It's not late! C'mon, loosen up, babe."

"Joe. Look, I'm not kidding. I'm tired and I want to go, *now*."

"Well, I don't. Nobody else is leaving."

"What?! Fine. *Fine*. Stay here then. *I'm* going back to the room."

"Fine with me," he said with a drunken grin, "I'll see you later."

8

‾‾‾

J ulie threw her slim beaded evening bag on the
dresser. *I'll be damned if I'll be here when he gets
back! That drunken sonofabitch isn't climbing in bed
with me tonight.* She picked up the phone and called the
service desk.

"Hi. This is Julie O'Hara, Deck 10, 1272. I wonder
if you might have a single room available? My partner
seems to be coming down with something and I don't
want to catch it," she said, kicking off her shoes and
slipping out of her dress.

Her face fell. "Are you sure? I don't care how
small it is or where it is. Please look again; I'd be fine
with an inside cabin." She scrunched the phone
between her left shoulder and her ear while she hung up
her dress. She was stretching the phone cord and the
handset pulled away. She caught it with her left hand.

"What? What did you say? Nothing at all?"

She sighed and said, "I see. Fully booked. Okay,
thank you."

Julie plopped in a chair in her underwear. Her arms were crossed and she stared straight ahead, her heels tapping a furious tattoo. *I won't stay here. I won't.*

She looked up. *I'll sleep in the spa. I'll find one of those double chaises with a mat.*

She found a pair of black Capri pants, a white tee shirt and an oversize crew neck sweater and put them on, along with her flats. She stuck her card key in her pocket and left.

A moment later, she re-opened the door and went into the bathroom, to her cosmetic case. *Where are they,* she thought, rummaging around in it. One package was for motion sickness. *Not that. There it is. Ambien. Thank God I got this prescription; I'd never get any sleep tonight without it.*

She slipped the pills in her pocket and hurried away.

———

"Where's Julie?" Adrienne asked.

"She left," Joe said. "She's a party-pooper. Dale left, too. Went to the Casino."

"Damn. I brought her book," she said with a dopey smile. "I wanted her to sign it."

"More like you wanted to make peace with her," Cathy said.

"Want to dance?" Joe asked, oblivious to Cathy's comment.

"Sure," Adrienne said, looking around the room. "Why not?"

When the bartender announced last call, Gill and Cathy declined and left Adrienne and Joe to party on. By two o'clock the band had been gone for some time and they were the only stragglers remaining in the faux-candlelit nightclub. The bartender, who'd had enough of them, finally turned the lights full on. Joe squinted, grabbed Adrienne's hand and led her out the door. "Let's go talk somewhere else."

"Talk" the bartender, Gabe, would later characterize as "drunken ragtime".

9

～

Julie had gotten off the elevator on Deck 11 - the Lido Deck - and walked through the deserted pool area. The expanse of empty white deck chairs reflected the eerie glow of the pool's underwater lights, and the silence of the place hung heavy on the salty air.

She was headed mid-ship toward Horizons, the long buffet-style cafeteria, remembering that the Solaria Spa was beyond it, up a short flight of stairs on Deck 12. When she got there, she found it locked-down and empty, save for a few folks cleaning up after the midnight buffet.

How am I going to get to the spa? The only way is through the restaurant. It won't do me any good to go back down and walk through the Promenade to the rear elevators. The only one that goes to Deck 12 is the one that goes right to the Top Hat club. I'm sure as hell not walking through there.

She stood back by the pool bar and looked around.

Wait, the jogging path probably goes that far.

Julie retraced her steps and climbed the pool area stairs leading to the Sport Deck on top. It was cloudy with very little moonlight, but she could see that the port side jogging path did, indeed, go back as far as the spa and there was a light slowly sweeping fore and aft.

The non-slip runner's trail tripled its width as it curved through Solaria's columned portico and headed back on the starboard side to the front of the ship. Two of the matted chaises Julie had remembered were placed, one each, on either side of the glass doors. The spa behind them looked closed, but Julie tried the doors anyway to confirm it. There was an outside cabinet on the left and she tried that, too. It was unlocked and contained white, waffle-weave cotton blankets.

Julie shook out one of the covers and plopped down on the nearest chaise. She was utterly tired, yet wound-up at the same time. In all of their time together, she and Joe had never had a fight like this, never had a *night* like this. There had never been any reason to doubt his love for her, but tonight she had come in a distant second to alcohol. What did that mean for the future?

Would the real Joe please step forward?

Fishing in her pocket, Julie pulled out the bottle of tiny pills, swallowed one and settled back. She tugged the blanket up to her neck and tried to stop thinking about Joe and worrying, a complete impossibility. She thought back to when they'd first met, how she'd initially disliked him, had avoided and rebuffed him. Of course, in retrospect she knew why. *Because he was everything I wanted in a man, because I knew I could fall for him.* Letting Joe into her heart had made her vulnerable. The prospect of losing him now was more than she could bear.

Julie shivered and looked around. *Where's the moon?*

The overhang held a soft, recessed light, but it was too weak to fend off the dark, cloudy night. Julie wanted to get up and go back to the cabin, but the hypnotic sleeping pill was doing its job and lethargy was overtaking her body. Soon, she was asleep. It was a fitful slumber pierced with an ominous dream of turtles and a dark, flickering sea…a dream that vanished when she awoke.

Adrienne Paradis was also on the Sport Deck, smiling and swaying in the balmy Caribbean air. She stood with one hand on the railing, her eyes half closed in a state of epiphany. *Dale Gill and Cathy. Dr Sinclair.* How could she see so clearly now what she couldn't see before?

She smiled, opened her eyes and looked over the railing at the dark sea twelve decks below. The Mystral's lights danced and sparkled across the waves.

Tomorrow I'll set things straight.

But tomorrow was not to be, for in the next moment Adrienne's arms were flailing and she was airborne, falling headfirst into the night. As the surface rushed to meet her, synapses in her brain made a fleeting connection to baby turtles...

Moonlight on the water leads them into the sea...

TUESDAY

10

⁓

Julie had no idea what time it was when she opened her eyes. The sky was lighter in the east off to her left, but the sun wasn't yet over the horizon. She had a slight headache and wondered if it was from the wine she'd consumed. What was it, four or five glasses? Four: two at dinner and two at the Top Hat. Or maybe it was the sleeping pill.

Probably both. I don't think I'll take those pills again. I still feel tired.

The angry words with Joe in the nightclub came back to her. She was sorry about their fight. He didn't really fight, she reminded herself. *He just wanted to keep drinking. I better get back to the cabin. He may be worried about me. Or maybe he's not. Oh, hell, I'm worried about him.*

Julie folded the blanket and put it back in the cabinet and then made her way back to the elevators. Along the way she noted that Horizons had activity and lights on inside, but wasn't open yet for breakfast. *These crew members must get up in the middle of the night to prepare all the food.* Exiting the elevator on Deck 10, she passed her cabin steward, Miguel, who seemed to be on call twenty-four hours a day. *When does he sleep?* She wished him a good morning.

And then she stopped, not wanting to open the door. *What if he isn't here?*

She steeled herself for the possibility and went in.

Joe was there, all right. Fully clothed, sprawled across the bed, along with a few small, empty liquor bottles from the mini-bar. The rest of the single-shot empties were scattered here and there. Julie sank into the armchair.

What am I going to do? This ship is full of duty free liquor and bars. How can he possibly get sober here? Julie sat there looking at Joe, choking back a sob as tears welled in her eyes.

Stop it! This isn't up to you; it's up to Joe. You're not giving him enough credit! Orlando's full of bars and liquor stores, too. Joe is strong; all he needs is an AA meeting! Oh, God. That's what he needs. Do they have them on ships?

She picked up "Day Four" of the Mystral Bulletin, the ship's daily itinerary, wiping her eyes so she could read it. There was nothing in it about AA. *But that doesn't mean they don't have meetings. Why wouldn't they? This ship is like a city!*

Julie grabbed the phone and called the desk.

"Hi. Look…ah…I have a friend who needs an AA meeting. Do they have them on the ship? Right, Alcoholics Anonymous." *Please, God.* "In the Bulletin, under the founder's name? Okay. That's great, *great.* Thank you so much."

There it was, right on the last page: "Friends of Bill W. meet at 10:00 am and 4:00 pm, Deck 2, Conference Room A". Now all she had to do was stay close to Joe until ten.

Julie gathered the empty bottles and threw them in the trash. One by one, she took off Joe's shoes. When he didn't stir, she worked him out of his jacket, noting that he'd already lost the tie and unbuttoned his shirt. Then she stretched out next to him and put her arm over him.

I love you, Joe.

She was awakened by a tone, followed by the ship's intercom:

"PAGING ADRIENNE PARADIS. PLEASE JOIN YOUR PORT CHARLOTTE AMALIE GROUP, GANGWAY ON DECK FOUR. ADRIENNE PARADIS TO GANGWAY, DECK FOUR".

Julie realized they were docked in St. Thomas. She hoped it wouldn't make any difference to the "friends of Bill W." She got up and quickly washed, brushed her teeth and changed her clothes.

"Joe. Joe," she said, gently shaking his shoulder. "Wake up. It's eight o'clock."

"Hmm? Wha?"

"It's eight. We have to go somewhere, honey. Why don't you go get in the shower while I make some coffee? We'll have it out on the balcony, okay?"

"Okay." Joe pushed himself up to a sitting position and saw that he was still wearing his clothes. A heartbreaking look of guilt and shame took over his face. "Is everything all right?"

"Yeah." Julie said gently, "Go take your shower."

11

They found Conference Room A and knocked on the door. It was opened right away by a man who was wearing a tan ship's uniform. He was a big guy with an even bigger smile. Julie suspected that he probably had a big heart, too.

"Hi, can I help you?"

"I'm Joe. I'm a friend of Bill."

"Just you?"

"Yes. Just me."

"Woloomo, Joo. I'm Tom," he said, shaking his hand, his other hand resting reassuringly on Joe's shoulder. "There's coffee and a continental breakfast over there."

As Joe walked off, he shook hands with Julie. "Hi."

"Hi, I'm Julie. Should I come back later?"

"He's new here and we've got a large group. It might be better if I send him back up to you, okay?"

"Sure, I'll be in our cabin, waiting."

Tom smiled and closed the door.

Julie walked back down the hall and took the elevator to Horizons on Deck 11. A middle-aged couple got on at Deck 6. The wife said that they were going to the restaurant, too. "Guess we're the only ones who decided not to go ashore. We've been here several times and I *always* spend too much." They both laughed. Julie just smiled, lost in her thoughts about Joe. A tone sounded and the intercom came on:

"PAGING ADRIENNE PARADIS, PLEASE REPORT TO THE PURSER'S OFFICE, DECK FOUR. ADRIENNE PARADIS TO THE PURSER'S OFFICE ON DECK FOUR."

The elevator door slid open at Deck 11. Julie stepped out first and hurried to the restaurant, wanting to get back to the cabin soon for Joe. The wife was next, her husband on her heels. He grumbled, "I wish that woman would go to the purser's office," but his wife didn't hear him.

The long Horizons buffet-brunch was quite literally mouth-watering. The breakfast portion offered blueberry pancakes, Belgian waffles, lox and bagels, pastries, eggs any style, home fries, sausage, ham and bacon. Under live palms at the fresh fruit bar, giant watermelons were carved into tropical scenes. For those ready for lunch, there was roast beef and turkey, or fresh caught grouper, mashed garlic potatoes and a choice of several vegetables. And then there was the salad bar. And the pasta bar. And the dessert bar. And the ice cream bar.

Julie was oblivious to the bountiful display. She grabbed a tray and went through the line, picking a bit of this and a bit of that. At the end, a young waiter snapped her out of her reverie. "Let me take that for you." Julie followed him to a table just beyond a foursome who were seated next to the floor-to-ceiling windows. It was a lovely harbor view of Port Charlotte Amalie, with its emerald green hills dropping into the azure sea. "Will this be all right?"

"Yes, this is fine," said Julie absently, automatically taking her seat with her back to the couples at the next table. Because of their loud chatter, it wasn't long before she wished she'd selected a more secluded table. She picked up her egg and croissant sandwich and tried not to listen...which was impossible.

"They haven't found her yet?"

"No, not yet. They're searching every nook and cranny on this ship."

"Couldn't she have gone ashore?"

"No, of course not, they'd know that. Remember that first day when we stopped at that beach on Parrot Cay? They didn't just swipe the identification card. We had to look into the scanner so they could compare the picture and make sure it was us."

"Do you know the woman?"

"I don't *know* her, but I know who she is. She has that big travel agency; you've seen her ads in Boston, I'm sure. Paradis Travel?"

Adrienne Paradis? Julie thought.

"I don't think I know it."

"Well, I saw them putting up her picture on the Purser's desk, asking if anyone has seen her and to call if they have. They must think she jumped."

Jumped? Adrienne?

12

By eleven-twenty that morning, most of the Mystral's passengers had gone ashore to tour the island of St. Thomas, so the unusual number of plain-clothes security officers visibly patrolling corridors and knocking on cabin doors was as obvious as a hundred referees in an empty stadium. But the last thing Julie expected was two of them sitting in her stateroom. They both stood up when she looked in the open door.

"Good morning, Ms. O'Hara. Please come in. Sorry to intrude like this."

The speaker was a trim black man of average height with salt and pepper gray hair. He flipped open an identification wallet. "My name is Clyde Williams and this is Wesley Hall," he said, pointing to a younger man, an obvious muscular back-up. "We are ship's security officers. An American citizen, a woman, has been reported missing. We believe you and your travelling companion, Mr. Joseph Garrett, may have knowledge of this woman since you spent some time with her last night."

"Do you mean Adrienne Paradis? I've been hearing the pages."

"Yes. Could you tell me where Mr. Garrett is?"

"Well…yes. He's at an AA meeting."

Williams looked at his watch. "That should be over by now. Was he coming back here?"

"Yes. I think he'll be here soon."

"Perhaps we could ask you a couple of questions while we wait for Mr. Garrett?"

"Of course, but I don't really know Adrienne Paradis well. I just met her last night at the Captain's Table."

"Yes, we're aware of that," he said, looking at a small notebook. "Mrs. Catherine Byrne mentioned that. We are more interested in your whereabouts last night after you left the Top Hat nightclub."

"My 'whereabouts'?"

"Yes. If I may ask, where did you sleep?"

"Oh," Julie said, realizing there were probably closed-circuit cameras all over the ship. "You have me on video, don't you?" She didn't need an answer. "I slept in front of the Solaria Spa on a lounge. My companion and I had a spat."

"And what was the 'spat' about?"

"It wasn't about Adrienne Paradis, if that's what you're thinking. I was upset that Joe had fallen off the wagon. He's an alcoholic, but he's been sober for twenty years."

"And I'm starting on the next twenty years, one day at a time," Joe said as he walked in and put his arm around Julie. "What's going on?"

"These men are security officers, Joe. Adrienne Paradis is missing."

"The travel agent?"

"Yes, Mr. Garrett," he said, flashing his identification, "I'm Officer Williams and this is Officer Hall."

Julie immediately saw that they thought Joe had something to do with Adrienne's disappearance. They had accentuated their authority by not giving Joe their first names. Clyde Williams displayed a subtle change in posture. He moved his body ever so slightly so that, instead of facing Joe, he was talking to him in silhouette. Unaware, he was telegraphing his distrust by giving Joe the clichéd "cold shoulder". Wesley Hall's suspicion was obvious; the muscleman crossed his bulky arms and frowned the minute Joe walked in the room.

The contrast in their body language clarified something else: Julie was not a suspect. *But why are they focusing on Joe? He hardly knew Adrienne.*

"If you don't mind, Mr. Garrett, we'd like to ask you a few questions about last night. Ms. O'Hara has already caught us up on some of her movements after dinner. Can you tell us where you went after the Captain's Table?"

"Sure. I went with everybody else to the Top Hat."

"And what time did you leave?"

"I don't know what time it was," Joe said, looking at the floor.

"Do you remember who you left with?"

"No, damn it, I don't. You know where I just came from. I don't remember anything after going to the Top Hat."

"Where did you sleep last night, Mr. Garrett?"

Julie interrupted; she didn't like the way this interview was going.

"He slept here, Officer Williams. I can testify to that."

"I'm afraid you can only place him here at five this morning, Ms. O'Hara. That's when Miguel, your cabin steward, says you came back."

Joe turned to her, puzzled. "You weren't here?"

"I was angry," said Julie. "I slept on a chaise by the spa. It doesn't matter now."

"I'm afraid it does matter, Ms. O'Hara," Clyde Williams said, looking at Julie with sympathy. "We have a three-hundred-sixty degree camera in the Top Hat. Mr. Garrett and Adrienne Paradis were the last guests to leave the club shortly after two o'clock and, as far as we know, that was the last time she was seen on this ship.

"So my question, Mr. Garrett, is: What happened between two and five?"

13

A longer question and answer period with Clyde Williams, sans the muscle, followed in the Mystral's security office. The parrying back and forth produced no results, and finally Williams got down to his real concern.

"Mr. Garrett. We do not suspect you of foul play. We are aware that you, like Ms. O'Hara, only met Adrienne Paradis last night. We think that possibly there was an accident. If such is the case, it is unwise to attempt to cover it up. We know from the Top Hat video that both of you were feeling the physical effects of alcohol. The waiter said your conversation just before you left was disjointed and nonsensical.

"We also feel that Ms. Paradis must have fallen overboard from the top deck, Deck 12, the same deck as the Top Hat club. Had the fall occurred on a lower deck, there is a much greater chance that it would have been caught on camera.

"It's not at all uncommon for passengers to stand at the ship's railing and look at the moonlight after a night of drinking and dancing, Mr. Garrett. Is that what happened?"

"Look, Officer Williams, I admit I was blotto last night. If anyone was in danger of accidentally falling overboard, it was me. But I honestly don't recall being anywhere out on deck, with or without Adrienne Paradis. I might remember more in a day or two; I'll certainly try. That poor woman; what are the chances of finding her?"

The former military man sighed, releasing his previous idea of Joe's involvement.

"Call me Clyde. The odds aren't good, Joe."

"You mentioned cameras, Clyde. How is it the ship has a three-hundred-sixty-degree camera in the Top Hat and none on the railings?"

"We've got those in the public areas and on the lower decks. On top, we have panning cameras hanging from each bridge wing to survey our flanks, port and starboard. Her fall isn't on the video from the wing-mounted cameras; they could have just missed her. It was also quite cloudy and dark."

Julie was pensive, looking at Clyde. Joe knew that look.

"What? What are you thinking?"

"A couple of things don't add up. I got the impression that Adrienne was very familiar with this ship; that she'd been on this cruise before. Is that right?"

"Yes, she sailed with us a number of times," Williams said. "She certainly knew her way around the ship…but when one is drunk…"

"That's just it," Julie said, "I'm trying to figure out how Adrienne got drunk. When the waiter at dinner attempted to refill her wineglass – it was the Cabernet, I believe – she put her hand over the top of her glass and shook her head. I'm not sure that she even finished that first glass. She acted like she didn't like it.

"When we got to the Top Hat everybody ordered a drink, but Adrienne was more interested in dancing. She did end up with one cocktail while I was there. But then she left.

"I was surprised to hear that she came back. Did she drink more then?"

"No, we don't think so. She only charged one drink, a Margarita. But keep in mind, Adrienne Paradis was a small woman."

"There *is* another possibility," Joe said.

"A rufie," Julie said.

"What?" Williams asked

"Rohypnol," Julie said. "The date rape drug. Or scopolamine; it could easily be scopolamine, since it's prescribed in small doses for seasickness. They must stock it in the Medical Center. Did you say the bartender in the Top Hat overheard 'disjointed' conversation between Joe and Adrienne?"

Clyde Williams was leaning forward now, looking at Julie and Joe with new regard.

"Yes. Gabe Rossi. He said they were talking 'ragtime'. I asked him what he meant by that, and he said they were drunk and they weren't making sense. I see what you mean. While Joe could have gotten to that state on a whole day's worth of drinking, you don't think Adrienne Paradis could have gotten there on two drinks or less."

"It's hard to imagine, but you made a valid point. She *was* a small person.'

"Listen," Joe said thoughtfully. "I'm a private investigator and Julie is a body language expert. Why not let us help with the investigation, at least for the next few days?"

Julie nodded. "That's a good idea, Clyde. Joe and I barely knew Adrienne. We had nothing to do with her disappearance, and we have a social connection with all the people surrounding her last night who might actually have had a motive to see her gone."

"I sure wouldn't mind narrowing the field," Williams said.

14

⁓

The full-length mirror on the bathroom door was too fogged with steam to see and needed to be wiped with a towel. It seemed like someone else standing there, looking back…

I wasn't going to kill her, you know, but a person can only take so much.

It was her fault. She brought it on herself. Some people think they can do whatever they want to other people, but she went too far.

I'm not worried about Julie O'Hara. She couldn't have seen me; it was pitch black out there and I stayed in the shadows. I think I handled the Security officers well, too. When they came asking questions, I shook my head and looked sad.

I'm glad she's gone; she was a bitch.

Careful, don't think like that; it will show! You can get through this if you pretend it never happened. Pretend that someone else did it. Say it!

"It was someone else… someone else…"

15

The Mystral departed beautiful Port Charlotte Amalie in St. Thomas promptly at seven that evening. At eight, there was a public statement on the ship's intercom:

"ATTENTION. This is your Captain, Andrew Collier, speaking. I have an important announcement: This morning a thirty-eight year old American citizen, Adrienne Paradis-Simpson, was reported missing by her husband. When this passenger failed to meet her scheduled St. Thomas tour group, our crew and our security staff proceeded to conduct a thorough search of the ship. I'm sorry to report that we have been unable to locate this guest.

"Adrienne Paradis-Simpson was last seen in the early hours of this morning, did not return to her cabin and is officially declared to be missing. In the case of a probable MOB, or man-overboard, there are established procedures. First, marine regulations and protocol require that the United States Coast Guard and law enforcement authorities be contacted. That has been done. Second, the Mystral is cooperating in a full-scale search and rescue effort by modifying our itinerary and retracing our route.

"We apologize for having to cancel our scheduled port of Philipsburg, St. Maarten, but time is of the essence and the extra day at sea will allow us to search the transit area through the night and tomorrow. There will be extra lights during the night and we will be deploying our search and rescue craft.

"Please be assured that the crew is at your service and all on-board activities will still be available for your enjoyment. We will arrive, as scheduled, in Port Canaveral, Florida, at six o'clock Saturday morning. Thank you and good evening."

Throughout the night, whether it was in the casino, the lounges, the theatre, or anywhere else people gathered, the conversation was predictable:

"Didn't I tell you a woman jumped? She must have been very depressed."

"I heard she owned an international travel agency. She was rich. What did she have to be depressed about?"

Some passengers thought it must have been an accident:

"It was really wet on the deck last night, did you notice? I think she probably slipped and went over."

"You're right. I bet she did slip. Someone said she was drunk, too."

And then there were those who always thought the worst:

"You wait and see. Someone pushed her. Was she married?"

"Yeah, a young guy, a ball player."

"He did it. Wait and see. It's always the husband."

———

At midnight, Joe was standing on their balcony. Like so many other passengers on the Mystral, he was captured by the drama of the search swirling around the ship. With admirable efficiency, the life-jacketed crew had dropped flame floats and beacons. Rescue boats had been launched from port and starboard, with at least one crew member in a full immersion suit. A US Coast Guard MH-60 helicopter circled above, its powerful searchlights scanning the water.

Joe stepped back in. "Julie, come look at this."

She went out with him and they stood at the rail. "Can you believe this?" he asked. "A gigantic ship and four-thousand people, all stopped to search for one person?"

But Julie wasn't impressed, she was frightened. The trolling searchlight spotlighted a shark fin here and there, and was immediately devoured by darkness. No matter how she tried not to focus on that, there was a blackness out there that swallowed everything beyond the Mystral. Her latent fear of the sea came roaring back and Julie backed away from the railing, which suddenly seemed like the edge of a cliff.

For a moment, it had felt like Adrienne was standing there with her.

"I'm going to bed." Julie shivered and quickly ducked inside.

16

Adrienne was no longer in a physical body, but was an amorphous presence in a void where infinite dots of light were coalescing and taking shape. The shapes were coming and going, evolving in a way that Adrienne found intensely desirable.

Oh, how she wanted to go with them! She was composed of the same dots of light...but unlike the others, she was not changing and moving on.

She was paused as "Adrienne", a person who had been pushed out of her life too soon, abandoned like a small child at a stopover on a highway. She had not matured...her relationships hadn't reconciled...and her death was unjustified. Worse, she found herself tied to the place of her untimely death.

But fate had provided a surrogate who could help her. Adrienne's last powerful, random thought had reached Julie O'Hara, who was nearby in a receptive, hypnotic state. Julie had felt Adrienne's terror, had viscerally connected with her at that moment.

Adrienne could move freely above the ship or within it, but not away from it...and she did that, watching all that went on, particularly her surrogate...who had the power to set her back on her path.

For now, she would wait...in a cocoon with a ship named Mystral.

WEDNESDAY

17

It was nine-thirty in the morning, and Julie and Joe had gotten breakfast trays in the Horizons cafeteria and taken them outside to one of the empty tables near the pool bar, which didn't open until eleven. The summer sky was a clear powder-blue and a freshening salt-sea breeze ruffled the umbrella over their table. Julie tilted her face up to the sun. She closed her eyes, took a deep breath and smiled. Their paper napkins began to lift in the breeze and Joe gulped down his orange juice and set the empty glass on the napkins.

Their ship was cruising toward its home port, Port Canaveral, Florida, but very slowly. As usual, the Mystral's stabilizers kept the giant liner on an even keel, though a US Coast Guard cutter on the port side could be seen riding fairly large swells. The ship's own rescue craft were still combing the route as well, despite scuttlebutt that there was "zero chance of finding the MOB" at this point in the search.

Julie and Joe had been talking about home. They shared office space in Joe's refurbished family home on Lake Eola in Downtown Orlando, and they had spent the prior hour on their cell phones, checking in with their respective secretaries. Julie was especially concerned about her cat, Sol, an oversized Bengal who couldn't be let out because he scared the neighbors, who invariably thought Sol was an escapee from a zoo. Julie's secretary, Luz Romero, was staying at Julie's lakefront condo, looking after him.

"So how's Sol?" Joe asked.

"Aside from tossing around my pens and pencils on a daily basis, he's fine."

Julie kept them in a plastic mug on her living room desk.

"Merlin. The cat does that all the time. Why don't you just put them in a drawer? Then you wouldn't have to play pick-up-sticks every time you come home."

"It keeps him busy. Can you imagine what he might get into otherwise? I have to pick my battles with him," Julie said. "Did you talk to Janet?"

Janet Hawkins was Joe's investigative secretary.

"Yeah, I did. I asked her to get me as much info as possible on Michelle Sinclair. But what's your interest in the doctor?"

"I don't know, call it a hunch. I couldn't help studying her; there's an underlying, unreadable quality about Michelle Sinclair. She told Alice Kent she was from a small town in Maine. I think she said 'Heraville'. She looks as if she might be French, that's why I suggested Janet check out northern Maine near the Canadian border. We can chat up the Byrnes and Dale Simpson, but Dr. Sinclair is another matter. My gut tells me she had a problem with Adrienne. Also, I think she's involved with Captain Collier. When he turned toward her, I caught him preening a bit, straightening his cuffs. She tilted her head away from him, too."

"I get the cuff straightening. But she tilted *away* from him?"

"It was unconsciously sexual; she was exposing her neck to him. It's more obvious when a woman swings her hair over."

"Ah, yes."

"Don't get me wrong, neither of them was doing anything obvious. At first, I assumed it was just subtle flirting, but they were sitting a shade too close throughout the meal. Everyone has a personal zone reserved just for loved ones, you know? That's what I'm talking about. When someone 'crowds' you, when you feel like that, it's because someone is violating that private space. In my opinion, Michelle Sinclair was inside Andrew Collier's personal zone. As I said, nothing about it was obvious. I don't think passengers on a short cruise would pick up on it, but crew members might.

"And that means a frequent cruiser like Adrienne might have, too. What do you think the cruise line's policy is on a relationship like that? Could that have been a problem?"

"Good thought, Merlin. I'll call Janet. HCL must publish employment policies."

"I know Michelle had an intense dislike for Adrienne, Joe. Her expression changed the moment Captain Collier introduced Adrienne to the other diners, and even more so when Adrienne stood up to pitch herself and her agency. Of course, everyone thought that was presumptuous. Nobody else stood up when they were introduced, not even *moi*."

Joe laughed. "Right. If anyone should have taken a bow, it was you."

Julie grinned. "No, I'm serious. When Adrienne stood up, Michelle Sinclair turned and pulled her head back a bit; she also looked down her nose. They were barely noticeable, micro-expressions, but you know how I'm always examining everyone. I don't think anyone else noticed it."

"Bien sur," Joe said, "of course, my all-knowing-one."

"Touché. If I'm so smart, how come we're not in Paris?"

The ship's Medical Center had just opened its doors to the patients waiting outside. Doctors and nurses alike groaned as the crowd, sniffling and coughing, played musical chairs in the tiny waiting room, an inconsiderate display that left a woman standing with a cast on her leg.

"Here, please sit down," Michelle said, pulling a chair from behind the reception desk. "How are you feeling today?"

"I'm doing okay, Dr. Sinclair," the older woman said, "but I need some more of that medicine. My ankle's hurting."

"I'll get that for you right now. Did you bring the prescription?"

The woman handed her the script and Michelle headed into the pharmacy to get the medicine.

She was humming as she searched through the shelves. Dion Jimenez – a newly hired young doctor on his first cruise – was ogling her bare legs in her trademark white sling-back heels, when she suddenly turned around and caught him. "Yes, Dr. Jimenez? Are you looking for something?"

"Oh, no. Sorry. I heard you humming…just wondering why you sound so happy this morning? Seeing how busy we are and all."

Michelle grabbed the package of medicine and said, "The day goes by faster when you're busy, don't you think?"

Love has changed my perception of time, she thought.

Anticipation and excitement were new emotions for Michelle Sinclair. There'd been no joy in her childhood, no pride of achievement when she graduated college and medical school. And then, swiftly after certification, things went from bad to worse. Another step, another lie, another year, what did it matter? Time, without hope, simply passed...of no importance.

And then, at age thirty-nine, she was assigned to the Mystral and met Captain Andrew Collier. One year later and Michelle could hardly wait for nightfall.

Andrew won't have to be on the bridge tonight. No one expects to find Adrienne.

Two happy thoughts in a row.

18

J ulie had guessed right. She'd scanned the Adults'
Pool area for only a minute or so before she spotted
Cathy Byrne on a chaise, tanning with her hat over her
face. On the near side of the pool, Julie passed Lottie
Pelletier, the woman she'd met in the Windward
Lounge prior to the Captain's Dinner. Apparently
asleep with her knee up, she may have been unaware
that her bathing suit cover-up had fallen open. She was
very fit looking for an older woman, but the shocking,
shiny pink of an old burn scar covered most of her
upper thigh.

Oh, dear. Poor woman.

Julie continued stepping around pool bodies until
she got to Cathy.

"Hi, Cathy. May I join you?" Julie asked, simultaneously draping her pool towel over the chaise next to her.

Cathy removed her hat. "Oh, hi, Julie. Sure, sit
down."

"It's really warm today," Julie said.

Always safe to start with the weather.

"I know! I don't usually like the pool because it's too cold, but I've been in a couple of times already. It's salt water, you know."

"I didn't, but that makes sense. It's so blue; it looks like the swimming pool at my condo."

"Well, that's the Caribbean, isn't it?"

"Any more news about Adrienne?" Julie asked, angling herself toward Cathy.

"No. They don't expect to find her alive, I hear."

"Is the water *that* cold?"

"No, it's not the water. It's the fall…and the sharks."

That was dispassionate, thought Julie.

"It's so awful," Cathy said, upon seeing Julie's raised eyebrows.

Shit, I've got to watch my expression.

"Do you think she jumped?" Julie asked.

"Adrienne? No. I think she fell. She was really drunk."

"Did she drink a lot?"

"You saw her, Julie. She was bombed. Not to 'speak ill' and all of that, but look how she was with Joe."

"That aggravated me, I must admit. Joe doesn't remember anything, he was so drunk. That was very uncharacteristic …but there you are…'Life is like a box of chocolates'…"

"'You never know what you're going to get,'" Cathy finished the Forrest Gump quote with a laugh. "Except you *do* when it comes to men."

"I understand Adrienne came back to the club?"

Cathy paused, as if weighing her answer. "Yes, she brought your book. She wanted you to sign it."

"No kidding!" Julie said, touched that Adrienne would come back for that.

"No, she did."

"Security has been all over the ship. Did they question you and Gill?"

"Yes. We had a small problem; Gill went out for a walk. How about you?"

"Oh, worse than that. I was so mad at Joe, I spent the night in front of Solaria spa on a chaise."

"Gill said they think it happened on Deck 12. Did you see anything, or hear anything?"

"No, nothing. I took a sleeping pill, an Ambien. You could cook dinner on that stuff and not remember it. Thinking back, it was really stupid of me to take it and then go out on deck. I don't know what I was thinking. I'm lucky I didn't take a header overboard."

"Well, thank God you didn't. Oh, look, there's Gill," she said. He was wending his way through the deck chairs and lounges, tall and tan with thick silver hair, his open floral shirt lifting in the ocean breeze. He had a drink in one hand and a magazine in the other. He dropped the magazine on Cathy's lap.

"Hey, Julie, how are you?"

"Oh, I'm okay, considering…"

"Yeah, it's terrible. Everybody's shocked. I never saw Adrienne drink like that. She was always so…responsible.

You know what I mean?"

"Yes. She struck me that way, too. Have you been friends a long time?"

"Yeah, quite a while. She planned all our cruises, right, Cath?"

"Yes, we always went together," Cathy said, standing and putting on a wrap. "Gill, I'm getting hungry. Let's go get something to eat." She turned to Julie, tucking the magazine under her arm. "Would you like to come with us?"

"Oh, no, thank you. You two go ahead. I'm just going to relax here for a while."

As they walked off, Julie considered their disparate reactions. Gill apparently liked Adrienne, but Cathy certainly wasn't going to miss her. Julie settled back on the chaise, her eyes drifting across the pool. Lottie Pelletier was gone.

19

J oe had called Dale Simpson to express his sorrow about Adrienne and to apologize in case he'd been out of line the night before. To his surprise, Dale had welcomed his call and suggested they meet at Barrister's Pub on the Promenade. It was obvious that Dale's choice of meeting place and his method of coping with Adrienne's disappearance dovetailed. Hearing Dale's slight inebriation on the phone strengthened Joe's vow of abstinence. When he got to the small pub, he had a quick word with the bartender/ waiter, to omit the alcohol in anything he ordered…and then he took a table outside, so he didn't have to stare at the bottles.

Like most of the casual restaurants on the Promenade, Barrister's Pub was a sidewalk cafe. Although there were no other patrons in the bar, the ship's stores had plenty of activity on this "At Sea" day. All the duty-free shops were open – something that was not allowed whenever the ship was docked – and the

Promenade looked like an upscale, tropical Mall with liquor stores, designer boutiques, perfumeries, coffee/bakery shops and the like. Joe passed the time watching all the happy shoppers with their Mystral tote bags bulging.

He looked up several stories to the ceiling covering the huge area. It was made of translucent panels cleverly designed to resemble a vast skylight. Landscaped oases were carved out of the polished marble floor of the Promenade. *The artificial light doesn't seem to bother all these palms and plants,* Joe thought idly.

He glanced to the right and saw Simpson approaching.

"Hi, Dale," he said, standing. "How are you doing?"

The two of them shook hands.

"Okay, I guess, Joe."

"Hey, I'm sorry about Adrienne, buddy. Any news?"

"Thanks. No, there's nothing new."

They sat and waved the waiter over.

"They're not going to find her after all this time, Joe. I don't understand it. What could have happened when she left the club? How could she have fallen overboard?"

"I wish I could help, Dale. The truth is I got really drunk and went back to my cabin. I have no idea where she went when I left her."

Oddly, Dale seemed to accept that simple disclaimer at face value. Was it because Joe had just met Adrienne a few hours prior and had no reason to harm her? Or did he know Joe wasn't on the scene?

They were quiet for a moment or two.

"So, how long have you two been married?" Joe asked.

"Let's see, six years. Yeah. I'm thirty-two, so it's six years. I was playing for the Rays. We met at Tropicana Field in Tampa."

"Do you ever miss playing?"

"Yeah, sometimes," he shrugged. "The truth is they would have let me go. I thought it was better to take the money and run."

The waiter arrived and Dale ordered a vodka and tonic.

"I'll have the same," Joe said.

The waiter nodded at Joe. "Yes, sir, right away."

"Anyway, the timing was right," Dale said. "Adrienne needed me to woo the wives and keep them from feeling jealous. Besides, we had a helluva spark in the beginning, you know what I mean? I thought I died and went to heaven when I married Adrienne."

"So you two travelled with your clients a lot?"

"Yeah, the heavy hitters like Gill and Cathy. Especially cruises, Adrienne likes cruises. *Liked* cruises," he said.

Although Dale wasn't spelling it out in so many words, it sounded to Joe as if the "spark" had fizzled a while ago. "So what happens now? Do you keep working for Paradis Travel?"

"Damned if I know. I signed an agreement with Adrienne when we got married, but I don't remember exactly what's in it. Her folks live in Paris, you know. They're rich, wanted to make sure I wasn't after her money. Funny thing was, I really loved her. I didn't give a shit about her money."

Joe noted the past tense again and something that sounded like a pre-nuptial agreement. *Like hell he doesn't know what's in it.* "So, no kids, Dale?"

"No. Adrienne never wanted any; I did, but…"

But you're still a young stud and now you can have some, Joe thought.

"I could use some advice, Joe. The security cops think I did something to her. Hell, I was in my cabin the whole night, but how am I supposed to prove that? I was alone."

"I don't think that means much. So was I. So were a lot of people."

"You were alone? Where was Julie?"

"We had a fight. She slept in the Solaria spa, came back before dawn," Joe said. "We made up." Once again, he noted Dale's unquestioning acceptance of someone who got bombed with his wife and didn't have an alibi for the night. *Why doesn't he suspect me? I wouldn't be so trusting if our positions were reversed.*

"Listen, Dale, the problem you've got isn't just opportunity. Take it from me; I've been an investigator for a long time. When you get off this ship, what the cops will be looking for is *motive*. For instance, they're going to ask if Adrienne had insurance and who's the beneficiary."

"Yeah, I figured that," he said, frowning.

"So here's how it's going to go; pretend I'm the cops. Are you on her policy?"

"Yeah, but I never figured anything like this."

"Of course not," Joe said sympathetically. "The other thing they're going to look at is your relationship, Dale. I mean, if you two weren't getting along…"

"Hey, we had our differences like anybody, but we weren't planning a divorce or anything like that!"

Yeah, I bet the pre-nup ruled that out…

Dale picked up his glass and drained it. "This whole thing really sucks."

"It does. Sorry, man," Joe said.

"Oh, hell," he said, rising. "I've got to go. Paradis Travel has a shitload of unhappy passengers who want to make sure they get their refund for their cancelled St. Maarten tours. I've got to go check the list. Can you believe people are actually coming up to me and asking about that?" He shook his head. "I'll see you, Joe."

"Yeah, I'll see you. Just take it one day at a time, buddy."

Like me, Joe thought.

Dale Simpson went to the Tour Desk and checked the Paradis Travel list of guests against the list of those who had booked either the Phillipsburg Shopping Tour or the Explore St. Maarten bus tour. To his relief, every agency guest was accounted for by name and number of tickets. The Tour Desk assured him that all would be credited back the full amount they'd prepaid for the cancelled tours.

At least that was off his mind…"least" being the operative word.

Dale hurried back to his cabin, which was a complimentary mini-suite on Deck 10. Miguel, the cabin steward, had been there in his absence and cleaned everything. As usual, he'd twisted a beige towel into the shape of an animal and left it on the center of the bed. This time it was a dachshund adorned with tiny white plastic sunglasses. The stupid dog seemed to symbolize everything that was wrong. Dale snatched it off the bed and threw it against the wall.

He went to the bar and made himself another vodka and tonic. He put ice, vodka and then tonic in a short tumbler, looked at it for a few seconds, and then dumped the whole thing into a bigger glass, topping it off with more vodka. Grabbing the drink, he went to the sliding glass door, opened it and stepped out on the balcony. He sat on a deck chair and stared at the clouds that were gathering on the horizon. There were just a few white puffs, but somehow they seemed ominous. He took a deep, comforting swallow of vodka.

Dale Simpson was scared. In spite of all his planning to be free of Adrienne, there was no joy now that she was gone. On the contrary, Dale felt as if Adrienne was reaching out from her watery grave to clutch him and pull him in with her.

20

⁓

"**A**nything else you need, Captain Collier?"

"No. That'll be all, Captain Houghton," Andrew Collier said, quickly closing his computer screen. Alan Houghton was the Staff Captain, head of the Deck Department and second in command onboard. He would be on the bridge tonight, giving Andrew a sorely needed break. Ever since the MOB, there had been no rest for the Commander.

Always reluctant to share his personal life, Andrew didn't care to have people reading his email over his shoulder. This particular one was from his son, Kyle, twenty-nine, who was just beginning to understand the break-up of his parents' marriage fifteen years ago when Andrew was forty. His younger son, Jake, was unforgiving, but Andrew had hopes of changing that over time.

The divorce hadn't been Andrew's idea, but the sea was a jealous mistress. When he became a captain, the extra months away proved too much for Susan. At first, the mere thought of being permanently separated from his sons, who were only fourteen and ten at the time, cut to the quick, but he accepted his wife's decision graciously.

Although he was faithful with their support, the boys had refused to see him or even speak to him for several years. That was a terribly painful time, but now that they were older and more mature, especially Kyle, Andrew was trying hard to rebuild his relationship with them, albeit by telephone and the internet.

At least that's going well, he thought, considering recent events onboard.

As commanding officer, Andrew was acutely aware of his responsibility for the efficient operation of Holiday Cruise Lines' $800 million ship, Mystral. Paramount in his mind was the welfare and safety of the nearly four thousand people onboard. He had been absolutely sickened by the recent disaster involving the Costa cruise ship, Concordia, which had veered from of its approved course and run aground off the Italian coast, ultimately listing and sinking, with many lives lost.

The despicable behavior of the Captain – who had been drinking and partying with a young woman, and who then abandoned the ship prior to the passengers and crew – was unthinkable to a ship's captain like Andrew.

It was the reason Conde Nast Traveler magazine was aboard on this cruise. The Mystral and her captain had been chosen for a story that would counteract the terrible publicity generated by the Concordia. The spread would showcase a properly run ship and all that was wonderful about cruising. Of course, that was not happening now. Andrew had already called Valerie Gilman, the Cruise Director, and told her to cancel it.

But some things couldn't be summarily cancelled. With Adrienne Paradis overboard, quite possibly murdered, a full-blown investigation of everyone with any animosity toward her was inevitable. Andrew closed his eyes, his head resting on his hands.

Oh, Michelle. How can I protect you? What are we going to do?

21

⁓

J oe and Julie were having dinner at the Aussie Grille, one of the ship's small, elegant specialty restaurants. They'd chosen a secluded table and they were presently enjoying their main course, superbly grilled shrimp and filet mignon with asparagus. The problem was that they couldn't talk privately because of the over-solicitous staff. So far, they'd been visited by the sommelier, the headwaiter and the master chef.

"Thank you," Joe said, as the hovering waiter once again refilled his water glass. "We appreciate the wonderful service, but we'd like to be alone."

"Of course, sir, excuse me," the waiter said, smiling and backing away.

Julie smiled. "Funny how you have more privacy in a crowded hamburger joint."

"Well, I think they've got the message now. So, did you enjoy your afternoon in the sun?" he said, taking her hand. "And did I tell you how beautiful you look tonight?" Julie was wearing a strapless floral bandeau and white linen slacks.

"Thank you. But don't you want to know what I learned today?"

"Yes, but it doesn't trump how gorgeous you are."

"Good, I'm glad," she said, squeezing his hand. "Okay, here's the pool report. First of all, Cathy and Adrienne were only friends on the surface. Cathy didn't like her much and won't miss her. Gill Byrne, on the other hand, did like Adrienne, I think…as far as he's able to."

"What do you mean by that?"

"I mean that Gill is a self-centered man. He may be smart, but he has the emotional maturity of a twenty year-old. I think making money and taking risks are his drivers. I think he views life as a poker game, where the player with the biggest pile of chips is the winner."

"He digs adventure, no question. He's gone hunting in Africa and taken a trip up the Amazon." Joe laughed, thinking about it. "Gill even drops out of a helicopter to ski."

"So here's what I'm wondering, Joe: Why did he like Adrienne? A guy like him pals around with other guys. He certainly didn't care about her as a travel agent. That would be about as important to him as a decorator. Cathy was the one employing Adrienne's services; Cathy is the one who likes luxury cruises.

"Like you just said, Joe, this isn't Gill's kind of vacation. He's taken all these cruises to placate Cathy.

But how does an adventurer like him tolerate it? Well, he can gamble, for one thing. We know he does that. What other risks might he take? What else could he do to make a boring cruise more interesting?"

"He might screw around with his wife's friend, the travel agent."

"Bingo. That night at the Top Hat club, Adrienne was all over you; the two of you were dancing like it was a marathon. Dale and Cathy were talking about the meal we had and how great it was, but Gill wasn't saying a word. He was drinking scotch, one after another, and *scowling*. At the time, I thought it was the liquor."

"You think he was jealous?"

"Why not? You don't have to love somebody to be jealous. You only have to be possessive and immature. The fact that Gill is just as charming as ever doesn't negate the possibility that he might have given Adrienne a shove. Think about it: He's a handsome, wealthy thrill-seeker who goes through women like Kleenex. Guys like that lack empathy, and they don't take responsibility for their actions. And there's something else, Joe. I asked Cathy if Security had questioned her and Gill about where they were after the Top Hat. She intimated that they were in their suite all that night, but they 'had a small problem' because Gill had 'gone out for a walk'."

"You're saying that Gill is like a little boy smashing a toy so some other kid can't play with it? That's a leap for me, Merlin."

"Some little boys grow up like that, is all I'm saying. So what about Dale Simpson?"

"Dale's a bigger possibility, in my opinion," Joe said. He leaned back, his left elbow on the armrest. "There's a reason why cops usually zero in on the husband. Dale's got less of an alibi for the time Adrienne went overboard than I have, and he's got ten times as much motive."

"Correction," she said. "You don't have *any* motive."

"No. Security just thinks I'm covering up an accident. But you know what's interesting? *Dale* doesn't suspect me of a thing, even though I got drunk with his wife and was the last person seen with her. That's a little strange, don't you think? I can tell you right now, if our situations were reversed and *you* were missing, Dale would be answering some tough questions or bleeding all over the floor.

"Looks to me like he knows I wasn't there when she went over the side. You know why he wanted to get together? Because I'm a private investigator. He can't prove he was in his cabin when she went missing. He wanted me to help him figure out how to cover his ass."

"They didn't look like a happy couple to me," Julie said. "Adrienne ignored him, never mentioned his baseball career; she didn't even use his last name when she introduced him."

"They *used* to be happy, according to Dale. It sounded like a whirlwind romance in the beginning, although he didn't give up the throne to marry

Adrienne. Apparently, the Rays were about to let him go. Adrienne's parents in France weren't too happy about the marriage; they made sure he signed a pre-nuptial agreement. My guess is Dale would have gotten zip in a divorce, and then what would he do? He dropped out of college to play ball, and he wasn't that good at it. There's an insurance policy, too. I don't know the size of it, but he's the beneficiary.

"Look, here's a guy that was used as arm-candy, married to a woman who kept him on a leash to entertain her clients, a woman who probably cheated on him and never wanted to have kids. I'd say Dale's got plenty of motives."

"No wonder he's scared," Julie said. "If he did it, it couldn't have been premeditated, Joe. Surely, he would have seen what an obvious suspect he'd be? Maybe it *was* an accident."

"It doesn't matter. No body, no witnesses. Who can prove anything?"

As per Captain Collier's announcement the night before, all the ship's entertainment went on as scheduled, so after dinner they were able to catch the second show in the two-story Caribe Theatre. It was a terrific show with lavish costumes and sets, a performance that brought the audience to their feet. For Julie and Joe, it put all their cares on hold, as they laughed and clapped and got back into vacation mode.

They left just before the finale in order to beat the crowd to one of the elevators. The doors slid open on Deck 10 not far from their stateroom and they walked along talking happily, still in awe of one young woman whose soaring voice had wowed everyone.

Joe opened the door to 1272, but allowed Julie to enter first.

"Your cabin awaits, mademoiselle. It ain't Paris, but it ain't bad."

Miguel had set the stage for romance. The lights were low and smooth jazz played softly. The glass doors to the balcony were closed, but the drapes were drawn back framing the full moon, its silver path sparkling across the waves. Clean white, ironed sheets were turned back on the queen-size bed, the pillows plumped just so, a chocolate on each.

The ocean view beckoned and Joe slid the doors open to let in the sound of the sea and the warm, fresh salt air. They kissed and undressed each other slowly. When they were naked, Julie headed for the bed. "No, come with me," Joe said. He grabbed the extra blanket and led her out on the balcony. Pushing the deck chairs aside, he spread the blanket on the floor.

"Lay there, Julie."

She stretched out on the blanket, the moon and stars overhead.

"Is this like the 'mile high club' on planes?" she asked.

"Way better…"

22

B ob Sanchez, the Ship's Hotel Manager, was conferring *sotto voce* with Lana Medeiros, his trusted Head of Housekeeping, who also personally took care of the Captain's quarters. They were both tired after the rigors of the day, but felt that there were important things to discuss before they went to their respective cabins and turned in for the night.

In light of the recent Man-Overboard investigation, the issue at hand was whether or not they should reveal certain things…and if so, how much …and to whom?

For example, Captain Collier knew nothing about Ms. Paradis-Simpson's impropriety. As much as the two of them wanted to tell the Captain about it, they had both accepted "a little thank-you gift" from Mr. Byrne for their discretion, something that he would, no doubt, bring up, thus jeopardizing their jobs. Besides, the mere fact of a dalliance meant nothing, really, and it would certainly embarrass Mr. and Mrs. Byrne.

And then there was the issue of Dr. Sinclair, whom Lana had seen leaving the Captain's quarters in the early hours of the morning when the Paradis woman went missing. Not that that was unusual; Dr. Sinclair always left before dawn. But giving Security that bit of information would surely cost them their jobs. Plus, they really liked Captain Collier and had no desire to embarrass him, either.

It was a sticky wicket, but as crew members, they were used to keeping secrets, especially in their positions.

Mrs. Medeiros, who answered to Mr. Sanchez, was ultimately accountable for the care and cleaning of over eighteen-hundred cabins and suites. *Heaven knows* how many clandestine afternoon meetings and nighttime cabin switching she'd seen over the years!

And as for Mr. Sanchez? Most people couldn't possibly imagine the load he carried on his shoulders. Take weekly provisions for the restaurants, just *one* of his many responsibilities. Who could imagine negotiating for 65,000 pounds of fresh vegetables or 35,000 pounds of fresh fruit? Or 20,000 pounds of beef? Or 4,000 pounds of seafood?

Bob Sanchez did *not* want to get involved in this woman's disappearance. After all, she wasn't *here* complaining about an issue he could do something about, like a robbery…the woman was *gone*. Of course her disappearance was troubling, but it was an extra problem he didn't need. He came to a conclusion.

Adrienne Paradis-Simpson wasn't one of us, she was a passenger. I'm going to let Security handle it. They'll figure it out, or hand it off to US law enforcement and the Coast Guard.

"You know, Mrs. Medeiros, it's none of our business."

"Oh, I agree, Mr. Sanchez," Lana said with relief.

They said goodnight and went to their rooms.

23

Michelle arrived at Andrew's cabin at ten sharp that evening. He opened the door looking so tall and handsome that he made her heart sing. As usual, he quickly looked up and down the corridor. "Did you see Lana?" he asked.

"No, Andrew, but she knows. You can't keep a secret on a ship. Don't worry. The crew is happy for you."

"I suppose you're right." He took her in his arms and they kissed. "You smell *so* good. I missed you last night. Come, we need to talk." He took her hand and led her to the couch and they sat down. "I wanted to wait, to surprise you, but now I think I've got to delay my plan until all this mess is over. I'm going to ask HCL for permission to marry, Michelle."

"What?"

"If we were married, we could live together and work here on the Mystral."

"But how?" she asked, surprised. "They don't allow that unless you're in equal positions, Andrew. I thought they discouraged it even then."

"That's true, but they can do anything they want; it's not like they're bound by law. It depends on how much they value our service. Besides, you're independent."

Andrew was referring to her special status as an Independent Contractor, which allowed the cruise industry to escape any liability for its medical care. Other aspects of Michelle's unique situation as the Principal Medical Officer hung in the air, unspoken…

HCL's primary concern for medical care was cost. Personnel with dubious training often came from third world countries. US doctors with zero experience who would work for low pay were prized, with many being hired on the cheap before the ink on their license was dry. And if an experienced American doctor like Michelle Sinclair could be hired for the same price… well, HCL was only too happy to award three stripes and ask no questions.

"There's going to be an investigation, Michelle. It's already begun."

"Shh, don't worry, my love," she said, standing and soothing him. "Everything will be fine." She took his strong, bearded face in her hands and kissed him. He looked up at her and then put his arms around her, burying his face in her waist. She held him for a while like that, and then pushed him away gently.

"Come to bed, Andrew."

Michelle walked to the bed and began to unbutton her blouse and unzip her skirt. She removed them and laid them over the back of a nearby chair. She looked over at him, but he didn't move, obviously preferring to watch. She stepped out of her panties and placed them on the chair. Then she unhooked her bra and took it off, baring firm breasts with dark brown nipples. She draped the lacy bit of lingerie over the neat, white pile of her clothes … and then she stood there facing him, waiting.

He rose and came to her. "You are so incredibly beautiful."

They kissed deeply as she unbuttoned his shirt, slipping it over his shoulders and off. Andrew quickly stepped out of the rest of his clothes and shoes and they stood, skin sliding against skin, their bodies pulsing inside and out. He dropped to his knees in front of her, parting her and not stopping until she cried out. Then he lifted her onto the bed and they rocked as one, climbing the peak of their desire until they fell back, spent, on the other side.

He tried to speak afterwards, but she quieted him, knowing what he wanted to talk about, and knowing that it would steal their peace. Facing him, she held his hand until he drifted off to sleep. When his breathing was deep and easy, she rolled onto her back, careful not to disturb him.

As was her pattern, Michelle fought to stay awake, but eventually she succumbed to sleep herself. That was how she thought of it. Her body succumbed to the deep desire for rest, while her mind succumbed to overwhelming sadness and terror.

It always began the same way. The little girl said "Mama?" and the big woman said, "Cecile." The little girl didn't understand. The other women who came to the school to pick up the other children were all called "Mama". One day, when they were at home, the big woman slapped the little girl in the face. "Never call me that again. You are to call me 'Cecile'. And so, she never called her that again.

Still, even if she didn't like that name, that's what Cecile was, wasn't she? The little girl noticed that the Mamas liked it when their children drew pictures. They picked up the children and hugged them. Sometimes they just picked them up and hugged them for no reason, but she knew Cecile would need a good reason. So, the little girl drew very detailed pictures and colored them very carefully so she wouldn't go outside the lines. She showed them to Cecile hoping for a hug, but Cecile just said they were "very good".

They lived in a big, old house. There was a maid who came every day to polish things. She polished glasses and silverware, especially a fancy silver set on a silver tray. The little girl thought it was the nicest thing in the house; she could see her face in the big pitcher, just like a mirror. And there was another small pitcher, a teapot and a sugar bowl. The little girl wanted to play with them, to make believe she was serving tea, but she would never dare ask Cecile about that.

The other thing the maid polished was wood. No one ever sat at the giant table in the dining room that had so many chairs, but the maid polished it all the same. The living room furniture had cushions that smelled musty and made the little girl wrinkle her nose, so she didn't go in there, but the maid did. The couch and chairs had heavy, dark wood legs and knobs, and the maid polished those, too.

It seemed to the little girl that the whole house was dark: the floors and the paneled walls, the staircase and railings. She liked it better on the second floor where the bedrooms were. The floors weren't as dark there and the plaster walls were painted white.

But she didn't like the third floor…NO, NO…not the third floor!

She didn't mean to go there. Cecile told her not to go there and she wouldn't have. She only knew about the wide front staircase that came straight down into the front hall. She went up and down those stairs all the time, but only to the second floor. She saw them turn back and go higher, but Cecile said "never go up there".

The little girl would never disobey Cecile.

But these were different stairs.

The little girl found them by accident when she opened a door in the storeroom next to the kitchen. They went right up, turning round and round. She thought they would go to the second floor; maybe they were secret stairs to her bedroom! But when she opened the door at the top, she was in a room she never saw before and Cecile was there, sitting at a desk.

"What are you doing here?!"she yelled. She grabbed the little girl's arm and dragged her around the dusty, book-lined room. "This is Row Bear's room! How do you like it?" She shook the little girl and said, "Row Bear is dead, but maybe you should stay here tonight. Let him come and get you!"

Cecile released the little girl and pulled a skeleton key from the pocket of her dress. She locked the door to the back stairs, unplugged the single green-shaded lamp and, taking it with her, stormed out of the room through the other door.

The little girl heard the key turn in the lock on the other side of the door. She ran to it and grabbed the door knob, turning and yanking and pulling at it. She looked around fearfully; it was starting to get dark! She ran to the single, dormered window, but it was locked and painted shut.

Oh, what was she going to do? A dead bear was coming! Row Bear was coming!

———

"Michelle, you're okay," Andrew said softly, stroking her arm. "Wake up, sweetheart, it's a dream. You're here with me."

Michelle was breathing hard and there were tears in her eyes. "It was the bear; the dead bear was coming for me."

"It was just a dream. Here, I'll hold you."

She backed up to him. He put his arm over her and she held on to it. Safe in his embrace, Michelle thought about the nightmare, still frightening and vivid in her mind. Cecile had been talking about her deceased husband Robert Sinclair, who had turned the third floor of the old house into a small library. With her heavy French accent, "Robert" had sounded like "Row Bear".

"What time is it?" Michelle asked.

"It's midnight. Go to sleep, my love."

THURSDAY

24

⌐∿⌐

Julie was outside perusing "The Mystral Bulletin -
Day Six", which Miguel slipped under their door
every morning before dawn. She had just lowered the
itinerary and reached for her coffee when Joe stepped
out onto the balcony, razor in hand, half his chin
covered with shaving cream.

"I wasn't there when she went overboard, Julie."

"What? Adrienne? Of course, you weren't."

"No. I mean I *know* I wasn't. I remember! We were
standing at the elevator and I couldn't get it to work. I
was probably pushing the wrong damn button. I
decided to take the stairs down, but Adrienne didn't
come with me. There was a door to the deck right there.
She said she was 'going for a walk' or something. I

98

didn't care; I was looking for another bar! I went down to Deck 5, to the Promenade, but everything was closed. I remember seeing all those stores with their roll-up cages pulled down. Then I thought of our mini-bar and I came back here."

"I thought that's what you did," Julie said. "I threw out a lot of little bottles. There was cognac, scotch, vodka, Canadian Club and I don't know what else. The only thing you left was a couple of beers in the refrigerator. You had to be here awhile to drink all of that."

"You don't know what a relief it is to remember, Merlin. Clyde Williams had me worried with that 'accident' scenario."

"Well, I never doubted you for a moment. Speaking of Clyde Williams, you should tell him, Joe. By the way, we've got the day free; my interview with Conde Nast Traveler has been cancelled. It was in the Bulletin. Wonder when they were planning to tell me they had the art auction there instead?"

She stood up. "I'll pick up around here while you finish shaving."

"Okay. I'm starved; let's go to the buffet first." He looked at his watch, "It's only seven-thirty. We've got plenty of time. We can stop by Clyde's office before I go to AA."

Julie heard him singing in the bathroom and smiled.

They were in Horizons, their trays loaded with fresh fruit, bagels and omelets and Julie was teasing Joe. "What? No grits?"

Declining help from the waiter at the end of the buffet, they looked around for a table by the floor to ceiling windows. The restaurant was packed, especially the window seats where diners were watching the US Coast Guard cutter, which was still accompanying the Mystral.

Then Julie spotted Jon Reece, eating his breakfast and simultaneously typing on his laptop. With all his gear, he'd managed to hold down a window table for four, unchallenged.

"Hi, Jon. Mind if we join you?" Julie asked.

Clearly, he did, but it would have been bad form to refuse. "Not at all," he said, closing the laptop and setting it on the chair next to him. "Please, sit."

"I saw you cancelled our interview, Jon?"

"Not me, Julie. The Captain. Val Gilman, the Cruise Director, caught me before I left my cabin. You probably have a message on your phone, too."

"My publisher will be disappointed," Julie said. "No offense, Jon, but I'm just as happy to have the day free."

"None taken. I was just restructuring my piece. There's nothing preventing me from using guest interviews. I'm going to do a few more and write a story anyway."

Their conversation paused as a passing waiter poured coffee and asked if anyone wanted juice, which they all declined.

"Will you write about the Man-Overboard?" Joe asked.

"You bet! Conde Nast won't want it, but I don't care. I can sell this story anywhere. It's all anyone's talking about; who thinks she fell, who thinks she jumped. One guy I spoke with swears he heard a 'thud' on his balcony. Security checked, but they didn't find anything out there."

"It's tough to investigate when the crime scene floats away," said Joe.

"That's a good line; can I quote you?"

"I'd rather you didn't."

"No problem."

"So who will you sell it to?" Julie asked.

"Newspapers. News magazines. There's plenty of mayhem on cruise ships, among passengers *and* crew. What else would you expect with thousands of people onboard? Rape and robbery are the most common problems, but the industry keeps a tight lid on all of it. The cruise lines only report what they absolutely must and not one word more.

"A 'Man Overboard' is one of those things that have to be reported, but the incidence is downplayed. It happens more often than people think. Passengers get drunk and take risks, usually stupid things. They fall overboard playing games on their balconies or climbing somewhere dangerous with a camera." Jon took a sip of his coffee and lowered his voice. "The MOBs involving the crew are different, but even more hush-hush. You never hear about the crew member who deliberately jumps ship when he gets to a certain port, or the staff member who commits suicide, like the Indian girl that jumped from another HCL ship last year.

"Their missing person reports are notoriously incomplete. When anyone tries to get more information, the cruise line stonewalls, claiming to 'protect the family' of the deceased. Meanwhile, the authorities consider the ship's information 'voluntary', so they don't push it. Really, how can they?"

"What if a passenger is murdered?" Julie asked.

"Then I'd have an even better story. Do you think it's a murder?"

"I think it could be," Julie said.

"Next to impossible to prove," Joe said, munching on a bagel.

I don't know about that, Julie thought. "Do you have a cell phone, Jon?"

"You bet!"

25

The Mystral's Security office was on Deck 1, just below the conference room where Joe would have to be in a half-hour for his AA meeting. Clyde Williams welcomed them and escorted them into his inner office. He took his seat behind his desk wearing a look of frustration that Julie was beginning to take as permanent.

"Glad you have a moment to see us, Clyde. How are you?"

"Good as I can be, Joe. What can I do for you?"

"I wanted to see you because I remembered what happened the night Adrienne Paradis disappeared. The details started to come back to me this morning. I've been remembering more and more about it. She and I walked out of the Top Hat club together. I wanted to look for another bar, but she didn't want to do that. She said she wanted to 'go for a walk out on the deck'. I remember that I couldn't get the elevator to work and we went to the stairs."

Joe looked down momentarily, then at Julie, and continued. "There was an exterior door there by the stairs. Adrienne threw her arms around my neck and kissed me. She said 'good night, darling,' or something dumb like that. I just turned and headed down the stairs. That was the last I saw of her, Clyde."

"I got off at Deck 5, but I couldn't find a bar that was open. Everything on the Promenade was closed with the gates pulled down, so I went back to our suite and raided the mini-bar. And that's it, I swear. I finished my binge and I went to sleep."

"I believe you, Joe. We don't have cameras on the elevators, so the only record we had of you and Ms. Paradis was a video of the two of you exiting the Top Hat club together. But yesterday we went over all the ship's video from that night and one of the 360 degree cams over the Promenade had you in front of Barrister's Pub alone at two-thirty. You were looking as if you wanted to go in. The pub, as you said, had the security gate pulled down. I'm inclined to believe that you did go back to your cabin from there."

Julie was relieved. She said, "What about the video from Deck 12? Anything new show up there?"

"No. As I said, the bridge-mounted cameras pan the port and starboard flanks. We've studied the railings on all the video and, other than you walking along, there's simply no one there after one in the morning. She had to have jumped around two-fifteen, immediately after she left you, Joe, and just after the camera passed, otherwise we would have caught her somewhere along the walkway by the railing.

"The ceiling mounted cameras on the outside lower decks didn't pick up much of anything that morning; it was too dark and foggy. The video shows the walkway and five or six feet past the railings...period. If anyone fell beyond that perimeter, the cameras couldn't pick it up because the visibility was near zero. We spotted a few passengers along the lower railings between twelve and one, and then no one after that. Not surprising, what with the fog and ninety percent cloud cover."

Julie was stunned. It sounded to her as if the investigation was *over*.

"Then you're assuming that she was alone and that she jumped?"

"It looks that way, Ms. O'Hara."

"Call me Julie. I find that hard to believe, Clyde. Adrienne Paradis was self-assured and forward thinking when I first met her. And later, when she was intoxicated, I'd have to describe her as happy-go-lucky. What I'm saying is, drunk or sober, I don't see Adrienne Paradis jumping to her death off this ship!"

"She could have fallen overboard accidentally," Joe said, trying to stem the tide of anger he saw rising in his partner. But Julie would not be sidetracked.

"I don't think an 'accident' makes sense, Joe."

She turned back to Williams. "Correct me if I'm wrong, but someone accidentally falling would be close to the ship, wouldn't they? Wouldn't some part of that person's body pass through the lower decks' cameras in that 'five or six foot perimeter' as they fell?"

"Maybe, maybe not. In this case, apparently not," he said, his eyes downcast and his face turned slightly away from them.

It was obvious to Julie that Williams was shutting them out. Was Jon Reece right? Had word come down from HCL headquarters to let it go, to 'sweep it under the rug'?

Before she could say anything else, Joe stood up, placing his hand under her arm. "C'mon, Julie. I've got to go. Thanks for seeing us, Clyde. Good luck with your investigation." Julie smiled and mumbled a hurried "thanks," as Joe steered her out of Williams' office.

As they climbed the stairs to the next deck, Julie said, "*Good luck with your investigation*? What investigation? Jon Reece was right, Joe. They're dropping it!"

"Maybe we should, too, Merlin."

"Over *my* dead body…"

26

The Art Auction in the Odyssey Lounge wasn't scheduled until late in the afternoon of Day Six, but the artwork was on display all day for potential buyers. Always an art lover, Julie decided to calm down and pass some of the morning there while Joe was at his AA meeting. She'd taken a quick tour through and was sitting at the bar sipping an iced tea.

Julie's best friend, the late Marcus Solomon, had been an accomplished artist and a good teacher. Under Marc's tutelage, Julie had learned what to look for, and she had acquired a small collection of fine art, some of which had appreciated nicely.

That was never going to happen with any of the overpriced artwork in the Odyssey Lounge, which was definitely not investment quality, as the brochure implied by referring to its "inheritance" value. As a collector, she had heard that such was the case in these "at-sea" auctions. Unfortunately, Julie could tell that most of the passengers admiring the art didn't know much about it. *They're duping some of these older folks with this crap. Retirees on fixed income, thinking they're doing their children a favor by leaving them fine art. The only "fine" that applies here is the amount they should levy on these auctioneers.*

"Oh, look, Phil. It's Julie!" Alice Kent led her husband through the crowd toward Julie. Her hands were full of materials kindly supplied by the scam artists running the auction: a brochure, a small pad of paper and a pencil. Julie saw that Alice's pad was full of notes.

"Hi, Alice, Phil. Are you going to the auction?"

"Yes, I think it will be fun," Alice said. "We've seen a few things we like."

"I do a little art collecting; would you like a couple of tips?"

"Please," Phil said.

Julie had to restrain herself from smiling. Phil Kent's relief was written on his face. Clearly, he wasn't the art lover Alice was.

"Okay. Number one: Slide your hand under the corner of a frame. No matter how nice it looks from the front, if you feel staples, it's junk. No one puts a valuable piece of art in a cheap frame, especially at an auction. Number two, get all the info: The name of the artist and the title, of course. Also, words like, 'hand-touched' or 'embellished' and 'signed', which is common, or 'autographed', which isn't. Take your list to the Internet Café, look them up and compare prices.

And remember, it's much easier to return something you buy locally, on land."

"That's good advice," Phil said, nodding at his wife.

"Yes, I suppose it is," Alice sighed. "Come on, Phil. I think I'll check the frame on that Thomas Kinkade lithograph."

Probably one of the priciest here, since Kinkade died last month.

"Okay, see you guys. Good luck!"

Julie turned back to her iced tea, smiling.

"That *was* good advice," the bartender said in an aside, as he wiped the bar.

"I had dinner with them the other night," Julie said. "They're nice folks."

"So are you. Julie O'Hara, isn't it?"

Julie looked at him quizzically. A tall fellow with sandy hair, he was wearing a name tag ...but *she* wasn't.

"Paul Gilman," he said, extending his hand. "I'm the Head Bartender on the ship. I worked this lounge during your seminar. My wife bought your book, *Clues*."

Julie shook his hand. "Nice to meet you, Paul. Your wife is onboard?"

"Yep. Valerie Jean Gilman, she's the Cruise Director."

"Oh, yes! Val Gilman," Julie said, remembering Jon Reece's comment about Val calling him to cancel their interview. "I didn't know married couples could do that, work and travel together on a ship."

"There aren't a lot of us; most of the crew is single. You have to interview and be hired separately, but as long as neither of you is subordinate to the other, there's no problem."

"Well, I guess that leaves the Captain out," Julie said laughing.

"Heh…guess you're right," he said, moving to the other side of the bar to wait on a customer.

Uh-huh, what have we here? A nice little cluster: a fake laugh, a tilted nod and a half-smile. The Head Bartender knows about Captain Collier's affair with Dr. Sinclair…and most of the crew does, too, I'll bet.

Julie saw Joe passing through the Photo Gallery on his way to meet her. She took a last swallow of her iced tea and said, "Good to meet you, Paul. See you later."

"Bye, Julie. Nice talking to you. Have a good day."

Julie met Joe before he got to the Odyssey. She took his arm and turned him around, heading for the elevator at the front of the ship.

"Joe. We've got to go back to our room and work out a new plan. We've left a very big stone unturned."

"Oh, no," he groaned. "I knew it. I knew you weren't going to let this go. What big stone?"

"I mean there's a whole *other* world on this ship. There are a thousand people in the crew who are single and married and live out of sight beneath the passenger decks. People who live in very tight quarters."

"So?"

"Gossip, Joe. Gossip…"

27

"I see two problems, Julie." Joe said, stepping into his bathing suit. "First, how are we going to get crew members to open up? Why should they talk to us? And second, we've only got a day and a half left!" He slipped his feet into his topsiders and pulled a white tee shirt over his head. "There are four-thousand people on this ship. How can we possibly find a killer in that time? It's a needle in a haystack."

"Okay. The 'four-thousand people' thing is bull, and you know it. Most of the passengers on this ship didn't know Adrienne from Adam! And I don't think any of her pampered clients wanted to kill her. So that narrows the list down to her husband, her friends and any crew members she had dealings with.

"Look, I just can't believe that Adrienne jumped off this ship. And the crew *sees* things, Joe. The security cameras are in some places, but the crew is *everywhere, all the time*. They're taking care of plants, washing floors, polishing glass and brass, day and night. The restaurants have people in and around them, either cooking or cleaning, day and night. And the poor cabin stewards! Miguel is *always* somewhere in the corridor; I think he sleeps on a pallet out there."

Julie had pulled on a pair of faded avocado shorts over her white tank-top bathing suit. She was looking around for her tennis shoes and saw them out on the balcony.

Joe followed her out. While she sat tying on her shoes, he leaned on the railing. The Mystral was moving at a good clip over a choppy gray sea, salt spray hitting the lower decks. Fluffy gray and white clouds raced past the summer sun, but out on the far horizon the clouds were heavy and dark. "Looks like rain."

He was thoughtful as he watched a pair of gulls, squawking and swooping as they followed the ship. "Getting information out of the crew isn't going to be easy, Merlin. They're trained not to talk to passengers about 'behind the scenes' stuff. I'd need to find someone who cares about doing the right thing, someone who would trust me to keep their information anonymous."

He looked at her for a moment.

"There are crew members in AA. I could go to the four o'clock meeting."

"That's a great idea. And I want to see Val Gilman." Julie had told Joe about her conversation with Paul Gilman, the bartender in the Odyssey Lounge. "I'm sure she'll be too busy to talk to me on the pool deck, but I'm hoping to set up a time to meet her later. It'd be great if we could do it while you're at AA."

Julie went inside, remembering that Val was supposed to have left a message. She looked over at the phone and the light was flashing. She picked it up and pushed the message button, then "speaker":

"Julie, it's Val Gilman, the Cruise Director. I'm sorry, but your interview with Jon Reece has been cancelled. It's nothing to do with you; we're delighted to have you onboard the Mystral! Everyone loved your seminar, including me! I'm told it's a question of space limitations. We have an art auction today and we need the Odyssey Lounge for preview space. Looks like you'll have more time to kick back and relax. Bye!"

"Well, that was a crock," Julie said.

"Might be a help. She may feel obligated to meet with you. C'mon, we should get a little pool time in while we can," he said, opening the cabin door.

He let go of the door to grab his card key off the bar. A gust of wind whipped through the open balcony door, slamming the cabin door with a solid *thwack*! "Whoa! What did I tell you? We're going to get a storm tonight!"

"You were expecting smooth sailing?"

28

Around noon, they went through the buffet in Horizons and took their sandwiches and iced tea out to the pool. It was much easier to find a table and deck chairs than on previous days, the sun-tan crowd having been thinned by the passing clouds and breeze. Another surprising change was the pool, where the salt water was rolling and sloshing quite dramatically.

"What's making it do that?" Julie asked.

"The Mystral is actually rolling; the water is staying horizontal."

"But it feels like the ship is level."

"It's not. The rolling is limited by the ship's size and its stabilizers, plus we've got our 'sea legs'…we're used to it, so it seems like we're not moving."

Joe stood up. "C'mon, let's go give it a try!"

After a few minutes in the pitching and swirling water, they climbed out, exhausted and counting themselves lucky that neither of them had been slammed into the sides of the pool.

"No wonder nobody was in there!" Julie said, drying her hair with a towel.

An older, gray-haired couple laughed heartily and called out to them. "We were wondering if anyone would be brave enough to go in the water!"

"They should cover it up," Julie called back. "Someone's liable to get hurt and sue them."

With that they laughed even harder.

"Are you kidding?" the man said. "I guess you didn't read the fine print. We signed away all our rights when we got on this ship. They're not liable for anything."

"That's right," the woman said. "I fell and broke my left wrist on the first day of a Mediterranean cruise. It was totally the ship's fault; it was a dark and slippery interior gangway. They ruined my vacation! I wanted to sue them, but no attorney would touch it."

The couple was getting up, preparing to leave. The woman held up her left hand. "See? I still can't close this hand; never will be able to, they say."

"Oh, I'm sorry," Julie said. "But you've forgiven them?"

"Oh, we do love cruising…all the wonderful food and being waited on, hand and foot. You just have to make sure you have plenty of insurance…and be careful!"

"Well, thanks for the advice," Julie called out to them, waving goodbye.

She turned back to Joe.

"These cruise ships remind me of something I read – I can't remember where it was – something about 'those who don't have the law are a law unto themselves'."

Just then she saw Valerie Gilman passing by the pool bar, clipboard in hand. She was about five-two, tan with short, curly blonde hair and blue eyes.

"Val! Wait up!" Julie called, wrapping her towel around her waist.

"I'm glad I caught you. Will my interview be rescheduled for tomorrow?"

"Oh, gee. I'm sorry, Julie, but, um, no. It was a space issue and, um…"

Julie cocked her head and stared at her. Val was a bad liar and both of them knew it.

Val frowned and sighed. "Oh, you know what the problem is, Julie. The Conde Nast article was supposed to be good PR for the Mystral, for cruising, in general. They can't let it go forward now. I'm really sorry."

Julie put her hand on Val's arm. "Don't worry about it. I really don't mind at all."

Val brightened right away. "Oh, I'm so glad! I'm a fan, you know."

"Yes. Your husband told me you bought my book. Listen, I'd like to talk to you about something. Are you busy now?"

"I am," she said, holding out the clipboard. "I'm hosting Bingo, from two to four o'clock in the Caribe Theatre."

"How about I meet you there at four?"

"Okay. Sure, I'll see you then."

"See you then," Julie said, turning back to Joe.

"How'd it go?" he asked. "Did the guilt-trip work?"

"Like a charm..."

29

⌐∽⌐

Joe stood at a wooden dais in the front of the room, grateful for something to stand behind and lean on. No matter how many times he would say this, it was always uncomfortable.

"Hi. I'm Joe, and I'm an alcoholic."

"Hi, Joe!" Twenty people in Conference Room A acknowledged him.

Five of the AA members were women and the rest were men. Tom, the big, uniformed crew member who led the group, presided from the back row on the right.

Joe, as a private investigator, was scanning everyone at this meeting with a new eye. Most of them seemed to be passengers, but he noted that two of the men, back row on the left, wore the Mystral's tan uniform pants and shoes, albeit with non-uniform shirts. They were strong-looking guys with weathered faces, taller than the many Filipino waiters and cabin stewards. He made another quick guess: *Skilled seamen.*

Tom, apparently noticing Joe's pause, gave him an encouraging nod from the back row. All the same, Joe appreciated it. It was never easy to bare your soul to strangers, and it was no easier this time. Like every addict, Joe had never believed other people when they suggested he was an alcoholic. It never hit home until he said it himself.

"I started drinking in High School and by the time I got to college it was a daily thing. But I kind of kept it in control, you know? My roommate, Sherman, and I were football heroes. We went to a state university and it was one big party." Joe shrugged. "Beats me how I graduated!"

Everyone smiled and laughed at that.

"Sherman and I had hopes of joining the FBI. Sherman made it, but I didn't. Of course, that made me feel *worse*, so I drank some more and eventually, I was such a mess I ended up in rehab…twice.

"My Dad's the one who came to my rescue. He'd been in the Navy, and he thought military life would straighten me out. So, as soon as I got out of rehab the second time, I enlisted. And you know what? It worked. I never drank while I was at sea, and I never touched a drop for another sixteen years. Not until three days ago."

Joe looked down and swallowed. He felt like he was back to square one.

"I got stinking drunk three days ago, my first day on the Mystral, and my first day on a cruise ship." He laughed, a short, disgusted laugh, devoid of mirth. "I'm at sea again, but what a difference! In the Navy, everything was in order, controlled, you know? But here...*it seemed like everyone was having a party*...I saw that and I wanted to party, too."

One of the crewmen made strong eye contact with Joe and nodded.

"Anyway, with God's help and AA, I'm sober again, one day at a time. I just wanted to say thanks to Tom and everybody else here."

Everyone clapped as Joe took a seat, an outside one next to the balding seaman.

"I know how you feel, mate. I have to look at it every day," he whispered.

"You work on the ship?" Joe whispered back.

"Yeah, I'm a mechanic. Name's Al."

They shook hands and were quiet for the rest of the meeting, giving the speakers the support they deserved. When the meeting was over, they were walking down the corridor toward the elevator. "They ever do tours of the engine room, Al?"

"They used to, not anymore."

"Damn! I would've liked that. Have you got time for a cup of coffee?"

"Well, see...the thing is, Joe...they don't exactly encourage the crew to mix with the passengers...except the officers, of course. Oh, what the hell, I'm off duty 'til twenty-three hundred…eleven o'clock that is."

Joe grinned, amused at Al's automatic use of military time. "Hey, you can take a guy out of the Navy, but you can't take the Navy out of the guy."

"You said it, mate," Al laughed. "There's a coffee shop this end of the Promenade."

They got off on Deck 5, where the shops were bustling with Mystral shoppers. Joe followed him into a Starbucks; they ordered two coffees and took a seat in the rear of the store.

"Would you rather take these outside where there are less people?" Joe asked.

"Nah. This is the best place, no crew around here at all."

Joe looked over at the three baristas serving up coffee.

"They ain't crew, ain't staff, either," Al said. "They're concessionaires. The shops, the Spa, the Photo Gallery, even the Medical Center, they don't work for HCL."

"So how do you like working on a cruise ship?"

Al took a sip of his coffee and smiled. "I like it. I've got a good cabin-mate; he's an older guy, like me. We go to the Crew Bar sometimes and hang out when the weather's nice. I get to travel all over and the pay's good.

"Captain Collier runs a tight ship, and the engine room is bright and clean as a whistle. Mostly it's light duty, too. Like tonight, I'm watch-keeper. I'll do a 'funnel to tunnel' inspection, all the levels from the top of the ship to the bottom, checking for leaks or noises, anything that might get by the monitors. The only thing is, it's bloody hot. "

Joe's eyes widened. "No air conditioning?"

"Nope. Hot as hell. The only place with AC is the control room; got to keep that cool on account of the computers and stuff."

"Whoa, I don't envy you that part."

"Hey, between you and me, there are a lot worse jobs on cruise ships."

"You mean like the cabin stewards? It seems like they never sleep!"

"Yeah, they work a lot of hours, even when we're in port, but at least they get tips. The ones I feel sorry for are the ones who do all the cleaning and polishing, especially the galley workers. Peeling, cooking and dishwashing to all hours. Can you imagine working sixteen hours a day for months?"

"You're kidding."

"Nope. That's the deal unless they're sick, and then they don't get hired again."

He looked around and lowered his voice. "Listen, they register these ships in places like Panama and Liberia where there ain't many laws. They hire workers from third-world countries who barely speak English, put four in a cabin and pay 'em a pittance."

"That's terrible!"

"Not if you're in their shoes, it ain't. It's a lot worse where they *live*. At least here they get clean quarters, good food and a little money to send home. Nah, they're grateful for the jobs. It's the ones who mix with the passengers who get upset every once in a while. Like you said, Joe, sometimes they want to join the party. That's why I'm happy to stay below."

Joe shook his head. "Some party, where a woman does a swan dive off the top deck."

"She didn't do no swan dive, Joe."

Joe leaned in, "What do you mean?"

"She had help."

30

At four o'clock Julie was sitting way in the back of the crowd in the big Caribe Theatre. She'd looked up and noted that the balconies were empty, but that was hardly the case on the main floor. The comfortable seats, which sloped gradually downward toward the stage in a wide semicircle, were nearly all filled with folks who had come to play Bingo.

It's the weather, Julie thought, remembering the sprinkles of rain that had started around two-thirty when she and Joe left the pool area.

Onstage, Val Gilman was calling out the last numbers of the game. An eager, young male assistant reached into a blower of spinning, numbered balls. With the wide-eyes and open-mouthed excitement of a mime, he retrieved one and handed it to Val.

"Could this be it? Could this be our big winner today?" Val said, drawing out the suspense. The players hunched over their Bingo cards, the old hands playing several at a time spread out on small cocktail tables.

Everyone was so silent and concentrated you could hear dust falling.

"B - Fifteen!"

"BINGO!" yelled a woman near the stage, waving her arms in the air.

"And we have a winner right here!" Val said. "C'mon up!"

Half of the passengers smiled and clapped, while the other half, disappointed, gathered their belongings and made their way up the aisles and out of the theatre.

"I almost had that!" a heavy-set man said to his wife as he trudged up the aisle.

"Ten cards. Ten effing cards," she said. "That's it, Frank. And I'm telling you, stay the hell out of the Casino."

Good luck with that, Julie thought.

Val Gilman was squinting and looking up at Julie, so Julie waved at her. She smiled, waving back. A few minutes later, she came and sat next to her.

"Hi! I hear it's raining quite hard. Did you and Joe get caught in it?"

"Hi. No, it just started when we left, about an hour and a half ago. Do you do this every day? The Bingo? They seem to love it."

"We have Bingo four days out of seven, but I'm not always here, thank God."

"I don't know how you manage everything, with events and stage shows and auctions and all. I can't imagine how you do it."

"With a lot of help! Let's see," she said, counting off on her fingers, "there's the musical director and the choreographer, then there're fitness, dance and golf instructors, counselors who handle activities for the kids, and then *so many* people who work under them. Onboard Entertainment is huge."

"Then you answer directly to Captain Collier?"

"No. The hotman is my boss." She saw Julie's puzzled expression and added, "That's short for the Hotel Manager, Bob Sanchez. Of course, he answers to the Captain. It's easier to understand if you see the ship as having two main employee divisions: The officers and crew that physically run the vessel, and everybody else. The hotman runs everybody else. "

Even though she was sitting only one seat away from Julie, Val was so bubbly and expressive that she used her hands to illustrate one group on one side, and one on the other. This was the second occasion on which Julie had observed Val's expansive gestures. Completely in sync with her speech, they confirmed two important things about the Cruise Director.

The first was that Val Gilman was an excellent teacher and a persuasive person. From her corporate training days, Julie knew that employees who could mentally connect large gestures to spoken words were far more likely to retain and 'buy into' information. Conversely, because Val's body language and speech were so naturally intertwined, it was tough for her to lie convincingly.

"Val, in your position you must know everything that's going on aboard the Mystral. What do you know about Adrienne Paradis?"

Just as Julie thought, the direct question left Val speechless and blinking. Before she could cement her "no comment" thought by voicing it, Julie persevered.

"Look, I know you can't volunteer any information on this, Val. I don't expect you to. I also know that you are a good person who wouldn't want to see a woman's death brushed aside like crumbs on a table, no matter what kind of a person she was. All I want to do is tell you what I already know. You can simply nod. If you do wish to tell me anything, I swear to keep it confidential."

When the Cruise Director said nothing, Julie took it as permission to continue.

"I applaud the Captain, the crew and Security for their exhaustive search effort. But after the most cursory of internal investigations, they are declaring this a suicide. Val, you and I both know that Adrienne Paradis didn't jump overboard. She wasn't the type, not by a stretch. And I know from looking up the statistics, that falling from a cruise ship is a rarity, and more apt to happen from a private balcony.

"Okay, so here's what I know from observing Adrienne, and excuse me for being blunt, but my time to help with this travesty of an investigation is short. Adrienne was flirtatious, but she wasn't 'easy'. She confined her extramarital activities to one person… Gill Byrne."

No argument. Val looked down, looked back up and gave a slight nod.

Yes! I knew it.

"That makes him almost as suspect as her husband, don't you agree?"

Another nod.

Julie looked away, pondering the situation, and then looked back.

"Here's something you may *not* know. I was with Adrienne most of that night, and I *don't* think she was 'drunk'." Julie consciously mirrored Val's expressive body language, using her hands to illustrate the quote marks.

"At dinner, Adrienne put her hand over her wine glass – like *this* – when the waiter attempted to fill it. It was half-full, Val. Later, at the Top Hat, she ordered only *one* cocktail, a Margarita. So, how did she get so wasted? Did you ever see her like that before?"

Head shake.

"So, the way I see it, someone slipped her rohypnol or scopolamine."

The Cruise Director was quiet, thoughtful.

"Val, is there anything you can add to this?"

"Perhaps," she sighed. "I have to talk it over with my husband. You have to understand, Julie. There are people who can't wait to take over *any* job on the Mystral, especially Paul's or mine. We aren't crew on this side; maritime law doesn't protect us. You stay silent or get fired. That's why most staff workers never complain about anything…ever."

"I understand; I promise to keep anything you tell me strictly confidential. I just need more information, Val. No one can solve a puzzle with half the pieces missing! We want to help, but Joe and I are running out of time. We'll be back in Port Canaveral soon and everyone is going to get off this ship and any semblance of an investigation will be over. No one's going to care what happened to that poor woman."

"You're right." She looked at her watch. "I'll call you in an hour."

31

J oe was waiting for her on the couch in their stateroom, his feet propped up on the coffee table; he was reading the Bulletin. Beyond him, rain pelted the glass balcony doors that separated them from the howling, gray seascape. Julie hurried past him and reached up to draw the drapes, to shut out the disturbing view.

"Well, hello to you, too," he said, tossing the Bulletin on the table. He got up and wrapped his arms around her and kissed her.

"I'm sorry, honey. I can't look at that; it scares the hell out of me."

"I know it does. Don't worry. When it comes to rough weather, the big ships are the safest."

"That's what they said about the Titanic."

"That was an iceberg. We're not likely to hit one in the Caribbean," he laughed.

"Don't laugh! There're thousands of little islands in the Caribbean. The Costa Concordia hit an *island* off the coast of Italy."

"Come here," he said, leading her to the couch. "I want to show you something that will make you feel better." He flicked on the TV to the ship's station. While soft background music played, a map of the Caribbean area showed the Mystral's progress toward Florida. "Look, babe, no islands in our path or anywhere near us."

Julie did feel better watching the ship's steady progress.

"You want a coke?" Joe had gone over to the bar to get himself one.

"Sure, thanks."

"They cancelled the Captain's Table dinner because of the weather. Did you hear the announcement?" Joe asked. "I'm sure Captain Collier needs to stay on the bridge."

"I didn't, but I'm not surprised. How'd you make out at the AA meeting?"

"I got lucky." He handed her a coke and pulled up a chair. "I met a marine mechanic. A guy named Al, who works in the Engine Room. You were right about the 'other world' below decks. It's kind of like a caste system, but skilled workers like him have a pretty good deal. They can go ashore and enjoy the ports, but onboard they can't fraternize with the passengers like the officers can. Al took a real risk, spending time with me. I got the impression that HCL is quick to fire people who step out of line."

"Did he say anything about Adrienne? Did anyone see anything?"

"Yes and no. You were right about the gossip, too. According to Al, nobody thinks she jumped *or* fell, Merlin, and for a very obvious reason." He shook his head. "If I was conducting an investigation under normal circumstances, I would have gone up there to Deck 12. I can't believe I didn't do that! If I did, I would have seen it right away. You probably didn't see it when you were up there because it was nighttime."

"What are you talking about?" she asked, leaning forward.

"The railing along the jogging track on the Sport Deck is made of clear, tempered glass panels with a single rail across the top. They're designed as windbreakers. It's way too windy on top for regular open railings, it wouldn't be safe. The railing up there is just like our balcony railing, only it goes all around."

"So what? I don't get it."

"Merlin, I'm six-four and our balcony railing is higher than my waist. Adrienne was short; it would have been up to her shoulders, at least her upper chest. You're tall, but you'd have to climb on a chair and hang on to the divider panels on the side to get over our balcony railing."

Julie pictured the jogging trail and the railing as it looked in the morning.

"You're right!" she said, leaning back. "There're no chairs and nothing to hang on to up there! And she was intoxicated!"

"Exactly. It sure sounds to me like someone helped her."

"Oh, Joe. They must *know* Adrienne Paradis was probably murdered. How can Captain Collier let it go like that?"

They were startled by the weird buzzing of the ship's phone. Julie grabbed it:

"Hi, Val... Not 'til tomorrow?...Oh, of course, sure...I understand. Okay. I can't tell you how much I appreciate what you and Paul are doing. See you tomorrow, thanks...Tonight? Yes, I think so... Oh, no, we won't; don't worry...bye."

She turned back to Joe. "That was Val Gilman. They can't meet us until tomorrow afternoon. They're coming here at four. She said she's extra busy because of the weather, plus her husband is closing the Top Hat tonight and opening the Odyssey tomorrow. She said Paul will be done for the day by four and she has two hours free then.

"Tonight's the last formal night, Joe. Val asked if we were going to the Captain's cocktail party or the Top Hat. I told her I thought we probably would. She asked us not to make any contact if we saw them; she said they can't afford to be seen talking to us."

"Incredible," he said, standing and shaking his head. "The *intrigue* on this ship..."

He went and opened the closet door. "We're going formal, then?"

Julie paused, thinking about the temptation that would surround Joe wherever they went. "Listen. Going out is up to you, honey. We can order in, just stay here and fool around. You're more important to me than this case, Joe."

He went to the couch and sat next to her, taking her hands in his.

"Babe, I know you mean well, but I can't hide from alcohol. Other people drink. Other people will be drinking in Orlando, too. For guys like Al and me, it's one day at a time, wherever we are. And for this one day, I'm not going to drink. So, let's dress up and go mingle with the suspects...and *then* we'll come back and fool around."

Julie smiled and began to unbutton her blouse.

"I have to wait 'til then?"

32

$\sim$

I t was seven-fifteen by the time they arrived at the Windward lounge, Joe in his white dinner jacket and Julie in a champagne chiffon dress. Val Gilman was standing at the door, welcoming people. Julie and Joe merely smiled, said "Good evening," and moved on by.

Once again, the chairs and loveseats were taken by folks quietly enjoying the classical music produced by a string trio, while everyone else mingled on the dance floor. Smiling waiters in black pants, white shirts and black bowties passed through the elegantly dressed crowd, their trays laden with cocktails.

As they made their way through to an open spot on the dance floor, Julie scanned the room looking for anyone they knew. Dale Simpson was nowhere to be seen, but Michelle Sinclair was there, along with Bob Sanchez, the Hotel Manager, and another officer. They were a striking group in their sharp white uniforms, standing in front of a wall-sized photo of the majestic Mystral. The officers took turns posing with individual passengers who literally put their best foot forward on the photographer's command. At the moment, Lottie Pelletier was having her picture taken with Dr. Sinclair. She was easy to recognize, wearing the same tuxedo-jacketed black dress. Julie's attention turned back to the three officers.

"Stand-ins for the Boss," she said.

"Yeah, we won't see him tonight."

She turned and saw the Byrnes coming into the lounge. She nudged Joe. "There's Cathy and Gill." Gill looked handsome in his formal attire, but Cathy was a red-carpet sensation. She wore an iridescent blue-green gown, strapless, slim and flared at the bottom. Julie caught their attention and waved. Gill returned the wave and they threaded their way through the crowd.

"Joe! Glad to see you," Gill said, clapping him on the shoulder. "Hi, Merlin. You look lovely tonight."

"Thank you, sir," Julie said. She smiled at Cathy. "And you look like a beautiful mermaid. What a perfect dress for a cruise."

Cathy beamed. "Thank you. I thought so, too. I was at Neiman Marcus and I couldn't resist it."

A waiter came by and they all ordered drinks, Joe opting for tonic water and lime. As they stood chatting, Julie picked up a change in the dynamic between Cathy and Gill.

Cathy was more secure. *No mystery there,* Julie thought, suspecting that Cathy had known about Gill's involvement with Adrienne, which was no longer a source of stress. Gill's body language, however, was puzzling.

He stood there with his arm around Cathy's waist. Julie remembered that yesterday they had walked part of the way from the pool to the Horizons buffet in the same awkward manner. She recognized it as a deliberate affectation on Gill's part because she knew that the side-by-side embrace was uncommon for anybody but younger, single lovers. Cathy, who was smiling and subtly rubbing against him, clearly didn't mind being newly joined-at-the-hip.

What's up with that, Gill? Are you trying to impress people with your togetherness?

"How's Dale doing?" Joe asked.

Before Gill could answer, Cathy blurted, "He's drunk. We just saw him at Barrister's Pub. I don't particularly want to be around him, anyway. Who knows what the real story is with him? They weren't getting along, you know."

Cathy's chin was thrust slightly forward and her eye contact with Joe had increased, her pupils dilated. Her defensive tone had all the congruent trimmings.

She accused Adrienne of being drunk. Now she's accusing Dale. Why do I think this smacks of misdirection?

Whatever was going on with Cathy and Gill, Julie was glad they weren't dining together. Joe had managed to reserve a table for two in the Main Dining Room, thanks to a cancellation. As far as Julie was concerned, the less time she spent with the Byrnes, the better; she had every intention of putting them out of her mind, at least for dinner.

Yet, the question nagged.

Why was Cathy defensive?

33

On the other side of the room, Michelle Sinclair looked over at Julie O'Hara and Joe Garrett and thought, *why can't you just leave this alone? Why do you need to ruin my life?*

Andrew had ordered Clyde Williams to stand down on the investigation into Adrienne Paradis' disappearance, and Williams had reluctantly complied. But Andrew had no way to control Julie O'Hara and Joe Garrett…and Security ultimately answered to HCL.

Michelle had done an internet search and learned that the pair had been instrumental in solving what had become known as the "swan boat" murder in Orlando, Florida. They had continued their tenacious investigation long after the police had pronounced the woman's death a suicide.

It was a disquieting thought. *Why have I drawn her scrutiny?*

Michelle had caught Julie O'Hara analyzing her the night of the Captain's Table dinner. Not once, but twice. The first time, it was so intensely uncomfortable that Michelle had felt as if she and Andrew were *naked*; she had instinctively moved her chair a bit further from him. O'Hara had seen through their public charade, of that she had no doubt.

But it was the second time that was more disturbing. Adrienne Paradis, her nemesis, had used her dinner invitation to stand up and make a sales pitch. It was galling, an insult to Andrew. *I couldn't help what I was feeling,* she thought. *I looked across the table and O'Hara was staring at me again.*

Michelle determined not to give Julie O'Hara any more ammunition. Apparently the fierce nature of her passion for Andrew was written on her face.

How ironic, she thought.

Cecile Sinclair had relentlessly taught Michelle as a child to suppress her feelings. If she was heard laughing, Cecile would appear out of nowhere, larger than life and scowling. "What are you doing? What are you getting into?"

Michelle would drop the toy, or whatever had delighted her, and cower in fear.

Anger replaced fear when Michelle turned fifteen, when she learned that the woman she had only known as "Cecile" was, in fact, her aunt. She would never forget that confrontation. "Why didn't you tell me,

Aunt Cecile?" she'd demanded.

In answer, she got a back-handed blow across her face that knocked her down.

"Don't ever speak to me again in that tone of voice, you ingrate! And don't call me 'Aunt'! We are *not* blood relatives. My husband was related to you, not me. I am fulfilling my duty to raise you. You will be a doctor like he was…or you can get out right now!"

Years of cowering had quickly snapped Michelle back in line.

She repressed all emotion for the next three years, psychologically protecting herself until she could leave for college. After that, they never saw each other again. Cecile never came to a graduation, even when Michelle completed medical school. Support checks and all contact simply ceased.

Michelle had been working as a doctor on the Greek island of Rhodes for two years when she heard that Cecile Sinclair had died. By then, Michelle couldn't risk going back to the United States. Not that it mattered…

They weren't "blood relatives".

34

⁓

Their table-for-two was against a low railing on the first balcony in the Main Dining Room. They were still one floor below the massive crystal chandelier which hung in the open center of the opulent dining room, but now they were looking down on the Captain's Table beneath it.

"I don't recognize anyone down there with the officers," Joe said, as he cut a thin slice of filet mignon.

"I wouldn't be surprised if they're folks celebrating birthdays and anniversaries like Alice and Phil Kent. They'd have to do something with that big table; that would make the most sense."

"This steak is great," Joe said, closing his eyes and savoring a bite. "How could you order plain old chicken?"

"This is not 'plain old chicken'; it's 'Soufflé Stuffed Caribbean Lime Chicken'."

"Looks like plain old chicken to me."

Julie, sorry that she'd ordered the disappointing chicken, cut a piece to spite him and smiled. She followed the bland bite with a sip of chardonnay, her eyes drifting around the huge dining room until they stopped at a small rail-side table on the opposite balcony. Lottie Pelletier was dining there, alone.

"I wonder if Lottie's a widow," Julie said.

"Who?"

"Lottie Pelletier. I was just wondering if she's a widow. She's the woman sitting alone across from us, on the other balcony."

"Do I know her?" Joe asked.

"I don't think you do. I met her in the Windward Lounge shortly before the Captain's Table dinner. You were in the Casino. I've seen her a couple times, but always alone."

"She's a nice looking woman. You'd think she'd want to sit at a group table."

"Oh, I don't know. Everybody's paired off on this ship, all couples. That would make *me* uncomfortable. The only difference is that I'd be reading a book. Frankly, there are a lot of times I prefer a book to company."

"Thanks a lot…"

Julie laughed. "Oh, c'mon, Joe, you know I don't mean *you*." She reached for his hand across the table and gave it a squeeze. "So, tell me, what did you think of Cathy's remark about Dale being drunk?"

"I don't know. It was weird. Definitely 'holier-than-thou'."

"I thought so, too. And the way Gill kept his arm wrapped around her, I'd say they've had a heart-to-heart since Adrienne went missing. They were closing ranks."

"Yeah, now that you mention it, it did look like that."

As they finished their meal, Julie reassessed Gill and Cathy.

Clearly, it was beneficial for Gill to keep his affair with Adrienne quiet, especially if he'd killed her; that might explain his sudden display of marital togetherness. But there was something about the way he was looking at Cathy…what was it? There was a moment of unexpected softness. When was that? Julie closed her eyes and recreated the scene…

He leaned over and touched her head with his…just for a moment.

It was spontaneous, a very personal contact…a loving contact.

"Oh, crap," she said, pushing her dish away.

"What? What's the matter? Something wrong with the chicken?"

"No, no, the food's fine," Julie said. "Joe, what if it was *Cathy* who pushed Adrienne over? What if it wasn't Gill, but Cathy? I'm sure she knew about their affair. When he left their suite that night to 'go for a walk', what if she suspected that he was going to meet Adrienne? She was terribly insecure, Joe. What if she went back to the Top Hat club? Oh, God, I hope that's not what happened."

Their waiter suddenly appeared in response to Julie having pushed her plate aside. He picked it up. "Is everything all right?"

"Oh, yes. I'm finished, thank you."

"Can I bring you some coffee or dessert? Some Black Forest Cake or Cherries Jubilee, perhaps?"

They both declined dessert and ordered coffee. When the waiter left with their plates, Joe leaned across the table. "So you think Gill's protecting Cathy?"

"I think it's possible. Suppose he loves her. He might feel he had a hand in it, that he drove her to it. Maybe that's what all this togetherness is about."

"I don't know, Merlin; I'm getting a headache from this," he said, literally squeezing his forehead. "We only have one more day on this cruise, and I'm willing to spend it trying to figure out what happened to Adrienne Paradis. I think there's no question that someone pushed her over the side. But, I'm going to say it again: *There's no way to prove it.* So, can we please forget about this, just for tonight? Let's go to the Top Hat, listen to some music and dance a little, okay?"

Julie reached across the table and took his hand again

"You're right. I'm sorry. Music and dancing it is."

"And fooling around."

"Especially fooling around."

It was Latin Night in the Top Hat club and the beat was infectious. Although the dance floor was crowded, there were a few Salsa and Samba pros who really knew their stuff. Intimidated, Julie and Joe sat and watched for a while, admiring their amazing hip action and fluid moves.

"C'mon," Joe said, holding out his hand. "We can do this!"

We can? Julie thought, following him onto the dance floor.

As it turned out, they could. It might have been a sexed-up Cha Cha with improvisations, but they moved their lower bodies in sync, and didn't sit until they were breathless.

They were resting on a loveseat downing a couple of cokes when Julie spotted Paul. He was working at the far end of the bar near a double glass door to the deck, which, in better weather, would have been open to outside tables. She nudged Joe. "That's Paul Gilman working the service bar, Joe. He's the tall one. The other guy was working here the night of the Captain's dinner. Do you remember him?"

"No, but he must be Gabe, the guy who said Adrienne and I were 'talking ragtime'. What an astute observation, huh?"

"Don't be sensitive, Joe. It was an important bit about Adrienne."

"Yeah, I guess it was." He set his glass on the small table in front of them and stood up. "I'm ready to call it a night, babe, how about you?"

"I'm ready; let's go."

They walked out of the club and were waiting for the elevator. Joe went over to the outside door just beyond the stairs and pulled it open a little, to get a feel for the weather. The wind was howling and it was raining hard; he shut the door quickly. "Can't go that way!"

The elevator door opened and they stepped in.

The non-stop glass elevator deposited them on the Promenade at eleven-fifteen. With the exception of Barrister's Pub and Starbucks, everything seemed to be closed. Music from the pub echoed through the Mall-like atrium, an upright piano with tipsy patrons singing-along. Although neither of them mentioned it, both Julie and Joe checked out the small crowd as they passed. Unsurprisingly, Dale Simpson was not part of the merry group.

By the time they got off the elevator on Deck 10, having walked the length of the ship from back to front, Julie was starting to feel woozy. Due to the high seas, the Mystral was rolling some and the movement was making her seasick. Oddly, she hadn't felt it when they were dancing. *With the music and all, I was having too much fun to notice it.* She was closing her eyes and clinging to the railing that lined the narrow corridor as they made their way to number 1272.

Joe was concerned as he opened the door. "You okay, babe?"

"Yeah, but I'm really dizzy. I need to lie down."

Miguel, wisely, had closed the balcony drapes. As usual, the mini-suite was inviting, with low lights, soft music, and the bed turned down for the evening.

Julie took off her earrings and dropped them on the bar. She slipped off her strappy heels and was fumbling with the side zipper on her dress.

"Here, let me help you," Joe said. Making no moves she might interpret as sexual, he unzipped her dress and unhooked her bra. While he hung up the dress, Julie, who often slept naked, stepped out of her panties and crawled into the bed like someone who had just crossed a desert and found an oasis.

Joe turned off the lights and the music, stripped and got into bed. He put his arm around her and lightly touched his lips to her shoulder. "Goodnight, sweetheart," he whispered.

In a little while she murmured, "I love you, Joe."

"I love you, too," he said, as the Mystral rocked them to sleep.

35

Adrienne drifted above the huge ship, unable to feel the earthbound whirlwind that caused the Mystral to dip and rock as it moved upon the water. It would not be long, she knew, before the ship would reach its turn-around point, the land-place where it would deposit the ones connected to her. They would go in different directions to finish out their lives. When the last life was complete, Adrienne's account would be balanced and she could move on.

That would be many Earth years.

The powerful longing to be free of the Mystral right now was difficult to control. She wanted to speak to her surrogate, to direct her. A voice tried to tempt her; it said those things were possible, that she could even possess Julie O'Hara if she chose to. But Adrienne knew in her soul that those who crossed that line were doomed to roam the sea forever.

She'd been given a gift. There was a chance that she might gain her freedom very soon. It all rested with her surrogate, with her ability to reconcile Adrienne's relationships and resolve the error of her untimely passing.

Adrienne would restrain herself; she would trust her surrogate.

But there was so little time…

FRIDAY

36

⌐◡⌐

J oe awoke at six-forty-five; the Mystral was still
rolling and he could still hear the muted sound of
the wind howling outside. *Shit. It's going to be another
lousy day.* To prove it to himself, he opened the drapes
a little and looked out. Big swells topped with white
stretched all the way to the horizon, a barely discernible
line between shades of gray.

He wondered if Starbucks had donuts. *Julie loves
donuts.* He looked over at her. She was lying on her left
side, the blanket clutched at her neck, her right foot
hanging over the side of the bed. He looked at her toes.
They were beautiful and sported a pale, iridescent pink
polish. He smiled. "Resort Pearl" was the name of the
color. He remembered the night he'd painted her nails

while she sat in a chair in a black lacy bikini. The polish was supposed to 'speed dry', but it wasn't fast enough. He'd wrecked her panties and her pedicure.

He looked down at the morning flagpole. *Forget it, you beast.* He turned and went into the bathroom. A couple minutes later, his teeth brushed and hair combed, he pulled on his jeans and a charcoal tee shirt and quietly let himself out.

Their ever-present cabin steward was two doors down. "Good morning, Mr. Garrett," he said softly.

"Good morning, Miguel. Is Starbucks open, do you know?"

"Yes, I believe it is, but they have coffee and pastries in the Central Lobby outside the Internet Café. The mid-ship elevator will let you off right there."

"Oh, that's great. Thanks."

"You're welcome, sir. Have a good day."

"You, too."

Joe headed off to his left. It was a long walk down a corridor of nothing but cabin doors to get to the mid-ship elevators. They had never used them because their stateroom was so close to the forward elevators and because the mid-ship ones only went up as far as Deck 10. He supposed they'd have to go this way for lunch. They could take the stairs up to the indoor side of the Horizons cafeteria on the Lido Deck.

Just ahead of him, Dale Simpson stepped out of his cabin. He looked horrible, almost like he'd slept in his clothes.

"Morning, Dale."

"Oh, hi," he said. "Good morning."

They turned the corner to the elevators. Joe pushed the button and the elevator door slid open right away. They stepped in and Joe pushed *Deck 4*.

"You headed down for coffee?"

"Uh, huh. You?"

"Yeah," Joe said. "Thought I'd bring some back to Julie. Tough night."

"You can say that again. My head's killing me. I used to be able to drink; not anymore. I went to bed with a headache and woke up with the same damn headache."

You're lucky, Joe thought. *You're in trouble when you feel so shitty all the time you don't know the difference anymore.*

The door slid open and they got off. Directly opposite, a long table was set up with coffee, tea, orange juice and, *God bless all things American*, donuts. Joe began fixing two large coffees, setting them into two corners of a cardboard tray; then he selected four donuts and put them in the center. He was putting lids on the coffee when he glanced over at Dale. In spite of the coolness of the lobby, the man had beads of sweat on his forehead.

"Dale, you don't look too good. Maybe you should go see Dr. Sinclair."

Dale laughed. "I don't think so. That's all I need! She killed someone, you know."

Joe almost spilled the coffee. "What? Where?"

He scratched his head. "In Maine, I think. No shit, she gave this broad the wrong medicine and she died. Why do you think she's working for peanuts on a ship?"

"How could they hire someone with that background?"

"Cruise ships like US doctors. Passengers like US doctors."

"Geez. You think the Captain knows?"

"It sure doesn't look like it," he said with a smirk. "Nah, he wouldn't have anything to do with vetting her. The medical staff is independent."

Joe had just tripped over a gold nugget.

"Hey, Dale, I've got to get back before Julie wakes up. Take care of yourself. Drink a lot of water; it'll help with that headache. The coffee will, too."

Dale raised his coffee cup. "Thanks, Joe. I will. See you later."

Damn, Joe thought, as he hurried back to their stateroom.

———

Julie was towel drying her hair when she heard Joe opening the cabin door. She smiled from ear to ear when she saw the tray. "Hi! I was hoping that's where you went!"

"I brought you everything you like and more," Joe said. "How are you feeling?"

"You are so sweet," she said, kissing him on the cheek. "I'm much better, thanks. Just to be on the safe side, though, I took some Dramamine." She looked at the donuts. "Is that chocolate glazed? Can I have it?"

"Of course. I got that one for you. Here, take your coffee, one sugar and half n' half." He handed it to her and they sat down around the coffee table. "Wait 'til you hear what I just found out from Dale Simpson," Joe said, munching on a jelly donut.

"What?"

"He said that Dr. Sinclair has a shady background, *seriously* shady. He said she caused some woman's death by giving her the wrong medicine."

Julie was wide-eyed. "How is she still working here?"

"Not *here*. It happened back in the States, in Maine. Apparently, cruise ship passengers like American doctors, so the company that staffs the Medical Center hired her. I don't think Captain Collier or HCL know anything about it," he said, reaching for another donut. "Anyway, the important thing is, if Dale knows about it, you can bet Adrienne did. She could have been blackmailing the doctor."

Julie sat back, sipping her coffee and thinking.

"Not for money, that's for sure. Adrienne was a control-freak, though. She may have used it to manipulate Michelle Sinclair in some way. Was she threatening to tell Captain Collier? Doctor Sinclair has access to scopolamine, too! She could have drugged Adrienne somehow during dinner…the wine…the food…I don't know, somehow."

"I've got a problem imagining a woman tossing her overboard, Merlin."

"I don't! Michelle Sinclair is tall and fit. Adrienne was a head shorter than her, not even five-feet tall, and she was small-boned, like a child. If Adrienne was stoned, how hard would it be to boost her over?" She reached for the phone.

"What are you doing?"

"I've been sick. I'm making an appointment with the doctor."

37

It was twenty minutes of eleven and the waiting room in the Medical Center was full to overflowing, most folks standing in line in front of a small sign set on the counter.

Are You Seasick?
Let Us Help You Here.

No wonder I couldn't get an appointment. Julie had come later, hoping to arrange a lunch meeting with Michelle Sinclair, but she hadn't considered how many passengers were sick from the stormy weather and the ship's constant rolling. *How am I going to get any face-to-face time with her?* As she was mulling it over, Dr. Sinclair stepped into the room, looking for a particular patient.

"Irene Serrano?"

A young woman with a splint on her finger stood up from a chair. Without giving it anymore thought, Julie beat her to it. She moved into Michelle's space, looked straight in her eyes and said in a low voice:

"Dr. Sinclair, I have to talk to you about something that happened in Maine. Something very confidential."

Clearly shaken, Michelle Sinclair blinked her eyes as if in doing so, Julie would disappear. But Julie stood her ground, separating the doctor and her patient. "Excuse me, Ms. Serrano," she said, resigned to the situation. "I'll be right back."

With admirable control, Michelle Sinclair calmly led the way out of the Medical Center with Julie on her heels. As soon as they were out of anyone's earshot, she whirled around, eyes ablaze. "What exactly do you want from me?"

Julie knew the value of putting on a confident front. She returned the stare, pulled her shoulders back and lifted her chin. "I know about Maine. I know about you and Captain Collier. I know you hated Adrienne. You can talk to me right now, or you can talk to Clyde Williams in Security."

It was a gamble, since Julie knew next to nothing about anything. One thing she *did* know: the first one of them to break eye contact would lose...

"I can't do this now," Michelle said angrily. "You saw the crowd in there."

"Of course you can," Julie said firmly. "You're the boss."

They glared at each other for a moment. Finally, the doctor closed her eyes, dropped her shoulders and sighed. "All right," she said. "I'll meet you in the

Odyssey in fifteen minutes."

Julie didn't exhale until the woman was gone…and then she sagged, amazed at her own audacity. *There's not enough time to go back to the stateroom,* she thought as she hurried to the elevator. She got off at Deck 4 and called Joe from the lobby, keeping her voice low:

"Joe, I did it. Michelle Sinclair is meeting me in the Odyssey Lounge in a few minutes. I can't believe I got her to meet me! The Medical Center was jammed; I think half the people on the ship are sick. Thank God I took my medicine. "

"You want me to come?"

"No. She hates my guts right now, but woman-to-woman is best. I don't know how long I'm going to be, but I've got a feeling this is going to be some story."

"All right. Don't drink anything, not even a glass of water!"

"Don't worry. The bar doesn't open 'til noon. I think that's why she picked it. It's a big place and fairly dark; we can sit out of sight there."

"Are you sure that's safe?"

"Oh, I think so. What could she possibly do? The whole front of that lounge is open to the main walkway and the Photo Gallery. Passengers are strolling by all the time and she's in uniform, very recognizable. Look, she wants to allay my suspicion, that's all. She figures all she has to do is keep me quiet for one more day. She plans to give me her best pitch…and I certainly want to hear it."

"Okay. I'll wait for you here. I'm going to try to get Janet, see what she's found out about Sinclair. If she's got anything, we can see how it squares with the doc's story."

"Okay. See you in a while," she said, hanging up.

Julie crossed the lobby and headed toward the front of the ship. She could see the Photo Gallery up ahead, busy with passengers hunting through the photo displays for their formal pictures taken the night before.

As she walked along, she tried to ignore the dark, violent storm raging outside the windows. It was impossible, like trying not to look at a bus full of people teetering on the edge of a bridge.

Happy, oblivious people, looking for their pictures.

Julie shivered at the unwelcome connection and quickly turned into the Odyssey, weaving her way through the club chairs and cocktail tables that filled the shadowy interior. The only lights left on in the lounge were recessed in the ceiling, casting a small pool of light on each of the curved booths that lined the walls. Julie slipped into one on the far right, positioning herself so that she would see Michelle Sinclair when she arrived.

She didn't have long to wait. The doctor showed up almost immediately, caught sight of Julie and slid in opposite her. "All right, I'm here," she said, angrily. "What do you want to know?"

"I'd like to hear your side of what happened in Maine."

"Why is that any of your business?"

"Look, Michelle," Julie said firmly, "you decided to tell me your side of things to keep me from talking to Clyde Williams, so let's not waste our time here."

Michelle slumped, her head in her hands.

"Oh, God, is this never going to be *over*?"

She sat up, inhaled deeply and willed herself to go on. "Obviously, you know what happened five years ago. What you don't know is how I came to work under an arrogant bastard like Dr. Jonas Howland in the first place."

"Start any place you like," Julie said, as if she knew who Dr. Howland was.

"I was raised by my aunt, Cecile. It's no exaggeration to say that she *hated* me."

Julie was taken aback. She was sitting across from a beautiful, mature woman whose face had suddenly transformed into the blank, unloved hopelessness of an abused child.

"I was a duty, a burden," Michelle said, "and Cecile never let me forget it. She was a widow and she must have done something awful to her husband, because she paid for my college and medical school as if she was clearing some terrible debt. She stopped supporting me when I graduated and I never saw her again, although I heard she passed away some time after that."

She closed her eyes for a moment, and continued.

"I trained at Monroe Regional Hospital in Bangor. Only a doctor could appreciate what that first year of residency was like! I worked crazy hours, sleeping in the hospital for days at a time. When the year was up, I was exhausted, broke and had nowhere to go.

"Then Dr. Howland, who had visited Monroe Regional a month before, called and offered me an extended residency at St. Simon's General Hospital in Portland. He said he would supervise me on a two-year specialist track in Internal Medicine, and that my hours and my salary would be significantly better. It seems so naïve now, but I was overcome with gratitude. I couldn't imagine that someone thought I was worthy.

"I was a fool, of course. His offer had nothing to do with my record as a doctor. I'm not proud of it, but I gave him what he wanted. I didn't love Jonas Howland, but I *did* love Internal Medicine and I didn't want to lose my position. To understand what happened, you have to understand Jonas. He was accustomed to *reverence*, to always being right. He misdiagnosed Anne Dunston, plain and simple. It was his fault, but he would never admit it."

"So what happened?"

"Mrs. Dunston was admitted in the emergency room and turned over to me, under Jonas' supervision. She was seventy and had previously been diagnosed with Fibromyalgia, but the only medication she was taking was Coumadin for Leiden Factor Five."

"Wait," Julie said, "I know Coumadin is a blood thinner; what's the other term?"

"Leiden Factor Five is a genetic variant that causes clotting, but that's not why she came in. Her complaint was that she hurt all over and she had a headache. She was running a very low fever and she had a brace on her leg. She said she'd fallen recently and twisted her ankle.

"It was the 'fall' and the 'Fibromyalgia' in her record that threw everyone off, including the unimpeachable Dr. Howland. We had her leg and her spine x-rayed, and had a cardiologist check her heart. Fine, fine and fine. We ordered a complete blood work-up and there was nothing remarkable except for an elevated SED rate."

"What's that?"

"The sedimentation rate. The higher number indicated widespread inflammation, which was undoubtedly causing her discomfort. Jonas said that referred pain from the sprained ankle had probably caused the general flare-up, a reasonable assumption for someone with Fibromyalgia. We couldn't give her anti-inflammatories because of her clotting problems, so he told me to order Percocet, which is Acetaminophen and Oxycodone, a mild pain reliever.

"It was late in the day, so with Jonas' approval, I kept Anne Dunston overnight. Four hours later, our patient...*my* patient ...had a massive stroke and died.

"She had been 'hurting all over' from Polymyalgia Rheumatica, not Fibromyalgia. What she needed was a high dose of corticosteroids to fight an immune system gone wild. That might have prevented the stroke. I say *might*, because it wasn't the Polymyalgia that caused it.

"You see, Anne Dunston had 'a headache' because twenty-percent of people who have Polymyalgia Rheumatica also develop GCA, or Giant Cell Arteritis, which restricts blood flow to the brain. That's what caused her stroke. It happened in the middle of the night; she died instantly, with no time to call anyone. The night nurse found her when she made her rounds.

"I was sick about it. I had to tell her husband, and it was heartbreaking. He was such a sweet old man and he depended on his wife for everything." Tears welled in her eyes as she remembered, and she paused and shifted her position to regain her composure. "As a doctor you have to get used to losing patients, Julie, especially the elderly ones. But it was the first time for me, and the thought that we might have been able to prevent it…"

"Did her family sue you?"

"Yes, her son, on behalf of the family. It took a while; he had two years to file a Wrongful Death suit, but I knew it was coming. I also knew that Jonas would lie to protect his reputation, so I left the country before they filed. I was in Madrid for a while, and then I went to work in a hospital on Rhodes."

Michelle sighed, "You might think living on a Greek island would be nice, but any island is confining after a while. When I found out that MediPro staffed the cruise ships that stopped there, I applied immediately."

"Didn't they check your background?"

"I never put Portland on my application, not in Rhodes, and not with MediPro."

Julie nodded. "So Adrienne knew and threatened to tell Captain Collier?"

"No, not Andrew. I told him months ago. It was HCL and MediPro that Adrienne held over my head, or *tried to*, I should say."

"You don't think they would they have fired you?"

"I don't know; maybe…maybe not. Andrew worried about it more than I did. I don't think Adrienne would have told them, Julie. She was overbearing, always wanting special treatment for her clients, but there was no gain in actually getting me fired. She liked the leverage of the *threat*. Do you know what I mean?"

Michelle's candor had won Julie over. She smiled and nodded, "I know what you mean. I saw it when she stood up and spoke at the Captain's Table. She held her hands in a palms-down position. It was a dominant gesture that said, 'you may be the Captain, but I'm the expert on this subject'."

"Yes, exactly."

Adrienne was so tiny, Julie thought. *Manipulation was a way to compensate…*

"Michelle, I don't know what to say. You've had a difficult time, but I'm sure you're helping a lot of folks on this ship. It was good of you to come. Thank you for doing that."

Michelle Sinclair raised her eyebrows and smiled.

"I had a choice?"

38

Julie's stomach was growling and she remembered that all she'd had to eat was two donuts. She wouldn't have thought so, given the movement of the Mystral, but she felt better when she ate something. Since it was lunchtime, she stopped and called Joe:

"Hi, I'm in the lobby. I just left Michelle and it's definitely not her. That woman's no killer, quite the opposite. She didn't like Adrienne, but she had nothing to do with her disappearance. Listen, Joe, do you want to meet me here? We could go to lunch."

"Sure. Where do you want to go?"

"Not Horizons buffet. I couldn't stand looking out those windows. Let's go to the Main Dining Room. I'm so glad I took that Dramamine; do you need some?"

"No, I never get seasick. I'll see you in a few minutes."

"Okay, bye."

The Main Dining Room was packed with queasy passengers who apparently felt the same way about Horizons. Julie and Joe declined the last remaining seats at a table for ten, and followed a uniformed hostess up to one of the third floor balconies for a private table.

The headwaiter, cleaned and pressed in a pale blue jacket, arrived and handed them the luncheon menus. Julie looked it over and was considering the blackened grouper, when the thought crossed her mind that if the weather worsened, a grouper might be considering *her*.

"I'll have the Southwestern Vegetable Soup and Club Sandwich, please."

"And you, sir?"

"The soup and sandwich sounds good; I'll have that, too."

They ordered iced tea and handed over the menus. As soon as the waiter left, Julie leaned forward and launched into an account of her meeting with Michelle Sinclair. Joe listened intently, and shook his head when she finished telling him about Michelle's patient, Anne Dunston.

"An elderly woman who had a stroke? You'd think that Internist would have just admitted to the diagnosis based on the information they had. It sounds like a reasonable mistake."

"I know," Julie said. "Howland had a distinguished background that would have carried some weight; the woman's son might never have sued *him*. He was willing to wreck Michelle's career so he wouldn't have a smudge on his."

"What a bastard."

The waiter came with a tray, setting it on a stand and removing the shiny, stainless steel cover with a flourish as he set each plate before them. *For heaven's sake,* Julie thought, *it's a sandwich and a cup of soup, not Pheasant-Under-Glass.*

When the waiter picked up his tray and stand and left, Julie remembered that Joe had intended to talk to his secretary. "Did you get ahold of Janet?"

"Yes, I did." He reached into his back pocket and took out a small notebook.

Julie smiled. *He's like Detective Columbo with that notebook.* She attacked her sandwich with gusto as he flipped through the pages.

"Okay, here it is. She confirmed Dr. Sinclair's med school graduation and two residencies, one in Bangor and one in Portland...nothing about any lawsuit, though. And the town you mentioned...she found a town called 'Herouville' on the Canadian border. Janet wasn't sure if I had said 'Sinclair' or 'Saint Claire', so she looked for both. Turns out the name 'Sinclair' is a shortened version of the French name Saint Claire.

"Ah, let's see...she found two brothers, both deceased; got information about them from two obituaries and a newspaper article. One brother, apparently, was better off than the other. Robert Sinclair and his wife Cecile owned a lot of property in the town."

"Cecile?"

"Yep. Must be Michelle's aunt."

Joe flipped the page and continued. "Robert died young; his obit said he didn't have any children. Cecile is deceased now, too; her obit didn't mention any children, either. The other brother, Marcel de Saint Claire, his wife, Nina, and their daughters, Charlotte and Marceline, lived in a cabin on Cecile Sinclair's property. According to the local paper, they died in a fire."

"Obviously 'Marceline' survived, Joe. For some reason, Cecile decided to change her name." Julie pushed aside the last quarter of her club sandwich. "That woman was cruel. I don't think Michelle knows anything about her immediate family."

Julie was pondering whether or not to give the information to Michelle, when her eyes came to rest on lone figure at a small table behind one of the balcony's supporting columns. The woman wore navy slacks and a white blouse, and she had draped a gray cardigan over the back of her chair. It was Lottie Pelletier.

"What was the other daughter's name?" Julie asked suddenly.

Joe flipped a page back. "Daughters, Charlotte and Marceline."

"Charlotte…*Lottie.*"

"Lottie?"

Julie leaned forward and lowered her voice. "The single woman who was on the opposite balcony last night. She's over there, behind the column. She has a large burn scar on her thigh, Joe! I saw it at the pool. I think 'Lottie' is short for Charlotte. And 'Pelletier' is

French, too. She's probably divorced or widowed."

"Michelle's sister?"

Julie thought for a moment and pictured Lottie quickly excusing herself to follow the officers, including Michelle, from the Windward lounge. She pictured Lottie again in the Windward, standing next to Michelle in front of a photographer. Michelle didn't see it, but Lottie's face was suffused with pride. And Lottie knew Adrienne.

"I think not…"

39

L ottie Pelletier was happy because Michelle was
happy. It was a wonderful feeling, to be near her
beautiful daughter on this beautiful ship. And to see her
smile! Lottie had waited so *long* to see Marceline smile.

Michelle, she corrected, *not Marceline.*

The unwelcome image of her father, Marcel,
intruded. Lottie's mood darkened almost immediately.
How she hated him, even now, forty years later!

After years of brutalizing her mother, he had turned
his attention to Charlotte. She was thirteen when he
assaulted her, fourteen when her baby was born. Proud
as a bull that had added to the number of his cows,
Marcel named his baby "Marceline".

Sadness welled up within her as Lottie remembered
her mother, Nina, who had suffered so much to protect her.

When Charlotte was a small child, Nina had covered
her with her own body as Marcel's blows rained down
on the two of them. After the rape, which shook Nina to
her core, she had slept with Charlotte and never left her

alone again; when the baby came, the three of them slept together. When Marcel, drunk, came charging into their little bedroom, her mother would leap up and distract him, take him from the room and satisfy him.

On the nights when that didn't work, Charlotte would listen to their battle. Nina would fight Marcel, tooth and nail, and the next morning Charlotte would help her with cold compresses for her bruises and bandages for her cuts.

The fire had started somehow on one of those nights. Had Nina's swirling bathrobe come too close to the fireplace? Or had Marcel, drunk, thrown a lantern? Charlotte, clutching her baby, only knew that something terrible had happened. She heard Marcel's awful bellow first, and then Nina, screaming and aflame, literally blew through the bedroom door, the fire behind her making a great *whoosh* as it swept in.

"Sortez d'ici!" Nina screamed. "Get out!"

Charlotte had rushed to the window, shoved it up and dropped Marceline out on the ground. She'd scrambled out behind her, her nightgown catching fire as she went. Charlotte had torn off the burning rag, scooped up Marceline and run naked through the woods to her Aunt Cecile's house.

Lottie Pelletier took a deep breath as she sat there, deliberately calming herself and reminding herself that she was a strong, fifty-four year old woman on a cruise…and not a burned, terrified slip of a girl stumbling through a forest.

She thought of her Aunt Cecile, about whom she had mixed feelings to this day. She had reluctantly hidden Charlotte and the baby, renamed "Michelle" by mutual agreement. But as soon as Charlotte's leg was healed, Cecile had pressed some money in her hand. *"Leave now,"* she had said, *"for the good of your misbegotten child."*

According to the deal she had made with her aunt, Lottie had left the small town of Herouville, Maine. But she never left the state, settling instead near Portland. She lived frugally, always saving half her income in the hope that someday she would get Michelle back. Periodically she would sneak into Herouville, just to get a glimpse of her little girl as she went from grade school to high school.

For the most part, it had been a hard and unhappy life. Lottie smiled a little thinking of her husband, Louis, a co-worker, who tried so hard to change that. He had called her "Lottie". Their marriage lasted only eighteen months, as poor Louis became aware that her burning love for her daughter eclipsed everything else.

Lottie had attempted to approach Michelle twice, at her graduations from college and medical school, and lost her courage both times. Thinking Michelle had been better off with Cecile, she had never realized how profoundly *sad* her daughter was until she got close to her on those occasions. Michelle never smiled; she had no affect at all, in spite of the celebration swirling all around her. And Cecile was always conspicuously missing, her contemptuous label, *"misbegotten child",* saying it all.

Afraid that Michelle would hate her, Lottie had kept her distance until now. A private detective had traced Michelle to Rhodes and, finally, to here, aboard the Mystral. Lottie was so proud of her! A doctor on a ship! She just had to come.

And Michelle was smiling all the time. Her child was happy…at last.

Lottie Pelletier would do *anything* to protect that happiness.

40

Joe sneaked a glance at Lottie. "Michelle Sinclair's *mother?*" he whispered. "No way."

"It's possible, if she was very young when she had her. It happens to thirteen and fourteen year-olds, you know," Julie said, keeping her voice low. "I noticed Lottie Pelletier having her picture taken last night in front of the wall poster of the Mystral, Joe. The photographer placed her sideways and slightly in front of 'Officer Sinclair', who was smiling her professional smile, the same one she wore for each passenger photo. But Lottie was *glowing* in way that makes more sense in this context…it was the love and pride of a parent posing for a family picture.

"Look, Adrienne and Lottie Pelletier were standing together talking at the cocktail party the night Adrienne was killed. Cathy Byrne introduced me to the two of them. What if Adrienne told Lottie that Michelle was not to be trusted, that she was a dangerous doctor? What if she said she was going to have her fired?"

"She'd have to be deranged to kill for that, Merlin."

"Not in this situation. Michelle Sinclair had a terribly sad, loveless life until she came to work on the Mystral and met Andrew Collier. If Lottie Pelletier is her mother and she's *here*, it means she knows that."

"So what now?"

Julie stood up, placing her napkin on the table. "I'm going to talk to her, Joe."

"How in the world are you going to do that?"

"I'll figure that out when I get there."

Joe knew better than to argue. "Okay. I'll meet you back at the ranch," he said, as he scribbled his name on the lunch bill and headed for the elevator.

———

Julie stood a distance behind Lottie. Softly, she said, "Charlotte de Saint Claire?"

Lottie turned around, a look of complete surprise on her face. And there was Julie, the only other person in that corner of the balcony.

She blinked and swallowed. "Are you speaking to me?"

"Yes, Charlotte. I believe I'm speaking to Michelle's mother, as well. May I sit?"

Lottie was dumbstruck, a look that quickly morphed into a smile of relief. "Yes. Please sit. How did you know?"

"I saw it when you had your picture taken with her. She looks like you, you know. And you looked like a proud parent, posing for a family photo. On the other hand," Julie said gently, "Michelle's smile and posture did not change, no matter who she posed with."

"You're right, of course." A look of long-accepted sadness hid like a ghost behind her eyes, even as a tentative smile played on her lips. "Thank you for coming to sit with me. It's nice to be able to talk about my girl. She's beautiful, isn't she?"

"Yes, she is, Lottie." Julie choked back her feelings. "I've gotten to know Michelle. I can tell you that she is as kind and as good as she is beautiful. She's a very good doctor, too. The Mystral is lucky to have her."

"Yes," she said with pride. "I don't tell anyone she's my daughter, but I ask them if they've met her. I've heard nothing but wonderful things about her! It makes me very happy. But I wish she would come back to Maine so I could see her more often."

Julie sagged with relief. Adrienne had said nothing to this woman! She thought back to Cathy Byrne's introduction: *"This is Adrienne Paradis and Lottie Pelletier. We were just talking about how much we enjoyed your seminar."* Lottie had left a moment later; she'd just been mingling at the cocktail party and chatting about the seminar, nothing more.

I wonder if she knows why Michelle left Maine…

"Is it safe for Michelle to return to Maine?"

"Yes, she can come back! That family sued Dr.

Howland! Two nurses came forward and testified that it was his diagnosis, and that Michelle was following his orders! I don't think she knows. I wanted to be the one to tell her…but I'm afraid."

She began to cry. Julie grabbed a napkin and gave it to her. "No, Lottie. That's wonderful news! And *you* are wonderful news…news that Michelle has longed for all her life."

Julie reached over and held her hand. "Maybe I can help. Will you tell me the story?"

And so Lottie shared her history for the first time since all those years ago with Louis. She told Julie about what her father had done, about the fire in the cabin and how her mother had sacrificed herself for Lottie and Michelle, who had once been called Marceline.

She reached for the napkin and cried again as she talked about her Aunt Cecile, about accepting the woman's terms for Michelle's sake. She cried about the graduations, particularly, about the terrible mistake she'd made in leaving her baby with that heartless woman! How could Michelle ever forgive her? Especially about her father…

"Lottie. You aren't giving your daughter enough credit. She's a mature woman, an experienced doctor. She will understand that a fourteen year-old orphan couldn't have taken care of her. She will understand what you gave up out of love for her. And she will know full well what kind of a hard bargain Cecile made, how she forced you out of her life. The fact that you are here is a testament to your love for her. She will forgive you, Lottie."

"But what about Marcel? How can I tell her that?"

"There's no need to tell her. You could say it was a young boy who moved away; that it was puppy love, a one-time thing. Who could contradict you? No one's alive, Lottie."

"Today's the last day of the cruise, Julie! How would I do it?"

"Come with me…"

41

When Julie slipped her card key into the lock of suite 1272, she was crying like a teenage girl at a three-handkerchief movie. Joe rushed over and put his arms around her. Naturally enough, he thought the ship's pronounced rolling was getting to her again.

"What's the matter? Are you sick?"

"No, I'm fine. It's Lottie Pelletier; it's been so hard on her, Joe," she cried. "All those years wasted!" She grabbed a handful of tissues from the bathroom dispenser and went to the couch, blowing her nose. "But they're finally together; that's what really matters."

"So I take it, it was her…but it wasn't *her*."

"No," she said, grinning through her tears. "Lottie's a good woman, just like her daughter. Oh, it was so wonderful, Joe." Julie couldn't help herself and started to sniffle again. "I took her to the Medical Center and introduced her to Michelle, and then I left the two of them. It was such a good feeling."

Oddly, Julie suddenly thought that Adrienne would want Michelle to be happy, too. *What am I, crazy? Adrienne did nothing but give Michelle grief.* Julie shook off the weird thought.

"I'll never understand why women cry when they're happy. Want a coke?"

"Yes…please."

"So we're back to Gill and Cathy and Dale," he said, handing her one.

They were slumped in frustration when they heard a soft knock on the door. Julie looked at her watch; it was four o'clock. "It's Val," she said, brightening and going to the door.

"Hi, Julie," Val said. Paul was behind her, a picture of resigned reluctance.

"Hi! Come on in."

Julie introduced the men to each other and they shook hands.

"Good to meet you, Joe."

"Same here. Can I get you guys something? We're just having a coke."

"No thanks, we're good," Val said, obviously nervous. "We can't stay too long."

Uh-oh. We better get down to business before she chickens out. "Please, sit down," Julie said, directing them to the couch. She took the chair opposite them, while Joe sat on the edge of the bed.

"Have you had any luck with your investigation?" Val asked.

Joe answered, "Well, progress of a sort. We know who *didn't* murder Adrienne."

"We were hoping you might have a lead for us," Julie added.

Val looked at Paul. He nodded, and she began. "We do suspect someone, someone who is about to be fired and put off the ship in Port Canaveral."

"How do you know that?" Julie asked.

"Because Paul's going to fire him," Val said. "It's Gabe Rossi. Gabe was tending bar in the Top Hat the night that Adrienne Paradis went missing."

Paul leaned forward, clearly uncomfortable.

"Look, let's get this straight. I don't think Gabe had anything to do with this Adrienne Paradis business. I caught him kissing a passenger, *not Adrienne*, on the outside deck of the Top Hat club after we'd closed. That was a couple weeks ago. He's always been a ladies' man, but passengers are off limits, so I reported him to the hotman."

Paul saw Joe's puzzled expression. "That's Bob Sanchez, the Hotel Manager. He left it up to me if I wanted to give Gabe another shot or not. I was inclined to forget about it because Gabe has been with me for over a year and he's a damn good bartender. But then this happened, and Val told me about Malaya …"

Val jumped in. "Listen, here's the problem. We can't prove anything we're saying here. Malaya is a server. She's this tiny girl from the Philippines."

Adrienne was tiny, thought Julie, alarm bells sounding in her head.

"Malaya won't talk to you or anyone else about this, Julie, but she told me she thinks Gabe raped her. She had a couple drinks with him at the Crew Bar. She said she thought he was 'nice and funny'. They left when she felt dizzy."

"Dizzy?" Joe asked. "Like drugged?"

"Yes. She doesn't remember exactly what happened. She thinks they went to his cabin, but she's not sure. She woke up in the crew's snack bar and there was blood on her skirt, and she'd lost her silver crucifix. When her cabin-mate noticed the blood, Malaya told her she had her period."

"Why didn't she go to the Medical Center?" Julie asked.

"She said it wasn't open, Julie, but the truth is she didn't want to lose her job."

"You mean they would fire her for being a *rape victim*?"

That was it for Paul; he wasn't going to say anymore. Valerie had persuaded him to come against his better judgment. He grabbed her hand and stood up, determined to end this thing. "The fact is they'd probably put both of them off the ship."

Paul opened the cabin door, ushering his wife out in front of him. Then he turned and said, "Look, things aren't done the same way here. If security catches somebody red-handed committing a crime, that's one thing. But if they just suspect someone, or someone's causing a problem, it's easier to put them ashore. That's what I'm doing with Gabe. End of problem."

Julie wanted to say *"for you"*, but she held her tongue.

42

G ill Byrne watched his wife getting dressed for dinner. It wasn't a formal night, this last night on the ship, but Cathy had tried on three outfits and still wasn't satisfied with the way she looked. This time she had paired a coral sweater with cream-colored linen pants.

"What do you think, honey? Do you like this? Do you think the lighter pants make me look fat?" She turned so he could see her derriere. She was barefoot and her pant legs, lengthened to accommodate platform heels, pooled around her bare ankles, accentuating her small, slim stature.

"Not at all. That's my favorite. You look beautiful."

Gill wasn't lying. He did think she looked beautiful, in a terribly sad way. Since Adrienne's death, he'd suddenly become aware of how emotionally and physically fragile Cathy was. *Why didn't I see it before?* His brain immediately provided the answer. *Because you were too busy thinking about yourself, you fool.*

I don't want another wife, he thought. *She's the best wife a man could have. I say "sign here," and she does. I say "I want to go there," and she goes. She does everything she can to help me, to please me.*

As Gill donned his sport jacket, he faced the fact that Cathy had always known about his cheating. *But I went too far, getting a separate cabin for Adrienne and me. There I was, waiting for my wife's best friend, like a stupid, horny teenager.*

Cathy must have left right after me.

Gill was *so* sorry. He loved his wife and he would stand by her.

Even if she killed Adrienne.

Cathy Byrne was bent-over in the bathroom, her long blond hair hanging down. She was spraying the roots with hairspray to give her smooth style more body. She straightened up, flipped her hair a couple of times with her left hand and gave it a final spray with her right. Being at sea, coupled with the stormy weather, made hairstyling a challenge.

That ought to hold it, she thought.

Looking in the mirror, she was reminded of her mother.

She looked a lot older than me when she was my age. She should have colored her hair. Just doing that would have made her look younger. And she smoked;

that breaks down collagen and causes wrinkles. Of course, they didn't wear sunscreen every day back then, and they didn't have laser resurfacing, either.

Not that her mother could have afforded that last one. Cathy's parents had divorced when she was twelve. Her father had moved to Texas, where he had remarried and had a second family...completely ignoring the existence of his first wife and child. Her mother had struggled financially for a few years and died of lung cancer before she hit fifty.

Cathy had promised herself on her wedding day that nothing would ever separate her from Gill. She knew from the outset that he wouldn't be faithful. It was part of the bargain, marrying such an attractive, wealthy man. Women threw themselves at men like Gill; expecting him to "just say no" was naïve.

Oh, yes, the affair with Adrienne hurt, especially when she saw how furious he'd gotten over Joe Garrett. Of course she didn't believe him when he said he was "going for a walk", but it was over now and her competition was out of the way. She would be the constant in Gill's life. She would be his safe harbor.

She would always have his back, no matter what.

Even if he killed Adrienne.

43

It was their last night at sea and everyone in the Main Dining Room was talking in fearful tones about Beryl, the monster tropical storm that was lashing the Mystral with seventy mile-per-hour headwinds as the ship slugged her way northwest toward Florida. With gusts up to a hundred miles-per-hour, Beryl was a hair's breadth from a category one hurricane and was scaring even the most blasé cruisers, who were gamely doing their best to put on a good face for terrified tablemates.

"Better to be on a ship than oceanfront on a beach. It's bad news when it slams into land. You can ride it out on a ship," one authoritative voice said.

Julie recognized the speaker, partly because his wife was seated next to him; they were the experienced older cruisers she'd spoken with after braving the pool. Julie smiled as she noticed that Alice and Phil Kent were seated at the same table looking like they wished they'd taken a train.

They followed their hostess onto the elevator which took them to the first balcony, where a rail-side table for two was set with all the Mystral's fancy tableware. Julie marveled at how nothing on the table seemed to be moving. Then the waiter came and filled their water glasses…just a little. Julie watched, fascinated, as the water level tipped slightly one way, then the other.

"So what are you in the mood for, Merlin?"

To hell with fish fear, she thought. "I'm going to have the pecan grouper."

Joe was looking at the menu. "Um, I think I'll have that, too. Are you going to have the onion soup?"

"Sure. It's perfect; the cheese will hold it in the bowl."

Joe was laughing when their waiter approached. He was a middle-aged fellow, mocha- colored with a cap of close-cut gray hair. "Well, I'm glad to see some happy faces tonight in spite of the weather," he said in a carefree Caribbean patois. "I am Rene. Are you ready to order?"

Julie felt herself begin to relax. "Yes, please, Rene. I'll have a Kendall Jackson Chardonnay, the pecan grouper and onion soup. "

Joe ordered iced tea and the same meal. After a bit of discussion, they added a Caesar salad to share and Rene left, promising to return shortly.

Julie leaned forward to keep their conversation private. "I've been thinking about Cathy. She's simply too small and frail to have hoisted Adrienne over a railing that high. Stoned or not, Adrienne would have been struggling, wouldn't she?"

"Sure she would; it had to be a guy. Someone strong enough to do it quickly. I don't like Gill for it, either. He had no reason to drug her. So, what do you think? Was it Dale or this guy, Gabe?"

"Well, Dale had opportunity and more motive than anyone. And do you realize I haven't seen him since the night of the Captain's dinner? It wouldn't be the first time a guilty party avoided me."

Julie stopped talking as she saw Rene approaching with their drinks and soup. When he left again, she resumed.

"From what I remember of that night, it could have been Rossi, Joe. I've been thinking about it. We were all seated together in the Top Hat and everyone ordered a drink at the same time *except* for you and Adrienne," Julie said. "You two were dancing when the cocktail waitress came to our table. You returned and caught the waitress as she was leaving, Joe. I heard you order a drink for yourself...but Adrienne went to the bar and came back with a margarita.

"She had plenty of time to flirt with Gabe Rossi. She may have flirted with him on other trips, for all we know. The way I see it, it was obvious that Dale and Adrienne weren't getting along; it probably was no surprise to Gabe when Dale left. And even if Adrienne was dancing up a storm with you, *I'm* the one you came in with. The odds were you would leave with *me*.

"So Gabe slips something in Adrienne's margarita, just in case she still wants to party after everyone else goes. What has he got to lose? He's closing up, alone. If he can get her to stay, he can have her right then and there. If not, so what? She goes home loopy.

"But, say it didn't turn out as planned because I left…and you stayed."

Joe nodded. "And when we finally did leave, Adrienne planted a serious kiss on me. We were in the hallway, right in front of the club and the doors were open. Maybe that was the last straw. Gabe could have followed her out on the deck after we split up."

A look of dead seriousness came across Julie's face. "That plays, Joe. There's a thin line between a man wanting to rape a woman and wanting to kill her."

They halted their conversation when Rene arrived with their meal.

The moment the waiter left, Joe leaned over and took her hand in his. "Julie. I'd like to nail Adrienne's killer as much as you. But there's no body and no witnesses. You know we're not going to solve this one, don't you?"

"Yes. I know. I can't stand it, but I know. We're going to dock at Port Canaveral tomorrow morning at six. According to the weather report, the storm will be in the Carolinas by the time we disembark at eight-thirty. And by five o'clock, the Mystral will be cleaned up, restocked with supplies, and three thousand new passengers will sail away, enjoying the sunset over

Florida. Who cares if a killer waltzes off this damn ship, free as a bird?"

"I care. There's just nothing we can do about it."

They ate in silence, neither of them happy with the inevitable end of their private investigation.

"Look who just came in," said Joe.

Julie looked down over the railing. It was Michelle Sinclair and Lottie Pelletier.

"If not for your digging, those two might never have met," Joe said, smiling.

"I am happy about that."

Suddenly, she thought of Gill and Cathy and their re-cemented relationship.

She felt an odd, warm happiness about that, too.

What the heck...?

44

*A*drienne saw Michelle Sinclair with her mother and was suffused with delight for the second time since she'd been in this strange, disembodied form.

It was an unexpected blessing that Lottie Pelletier was on the ship. Even if Adrienne had had the time to apologize to Michelle, it mightn't have been enough to earn her forgiveness. But, with just a little urging, her surrogate had brought the two women together, and now the doctor's happiness was sweeping away all ill feeling.

She had been delighted as she observed what was happening with Gill and Cathy Byrne, too. They were united as never before, standing together against the world. Adrienne knew that no apology from her could ever have accomplished that.

Still, her killer had yet to be identified.

Oh, he would pay the price when he came to the place where she was, the place where everyone's account was balanced. It was the comfort of her Earth *family and friends that most concerned Adrienne. They needed resolution; they needed his name.*

And Adrienne SO wanted to be free of the Mystral.

Julie must not give up! The answer was right there in her stateroom...

How to bring it to her attention?

45

It was seven-fifteen when Julie and Joe took the elevator down one level to Deck 4 and set off toward the front of the ship. They had decided to get their packing done, as all passengers had been notified in the Mystral Bulletin to leave their bags in the corridor before midnight.

They actually heard the bells and whistles and shouts before they reached the Casino. To their amazement, every slot machine was occupied, with eager onlookers quickly grabbing any available stool. While red velvet ropes kept spectators away from the busy poker tables, the roulette wheels and blackjack tables were surrounded by cheering would-be players who kept the cocktail servers busy while they waited for their turn to lose their money.

"Oh jeez, we'll never get through that crowd," Julie said, "it's packed in there."

Joe took her arm. "C'mon, let's climb the stairs. We'll walk through the Promenade."

The activity was only slightly less frenetic on the ship's main thoroughfare. Everything in the vast atrium was open and doing a bang-up business. The place looked like a Mall at Christmas, with shoppers' bags a-bulge. They passed by Finnegan's Café, where a trio of Irish singers were entertaining, while up ahead the usual bunch surrounded the upright piano at the cozier Barrister's Pub.

At the end of the Promenade, they went down the stairs, crossed the Lobby and walked past the Odyssey Lounge, where a pianist-comedian regaled the crowd.

"Well, I guess everyone took their Dramamine tonight," Julie said, astonished, thinking about the near-hurricane, Beryl, which was buffeting the Mystral, literally rocking the boat.

"It's a way to handle the fear," Joe said, "like sex. Which reminds me, how're you feeling?"

Julie laughed. "Eager. But let's pack first. I don't want them knocking on the door."

When they got off the elevator at Deck 10, there were very few bags in the corridor, which wasn't surprising, since everyone seemed to be having a hurricane party. They let themselves into 1272. The drapes were closed, the howling wind was muted and, given their own party plan, their bed looked even more inviting than usual. Nevertheless, they pulled out the suitcases and set about packing.

Joe finished the chore faster than a shopper on a blue-light special, stuffing everything pell-mell into his duffel bag. He left out a pair of briefs and shorts, a tee shirt and shaving gear for the morning. By eight o'clock, he was under the covers snoring softly, hugely irritating Julie, who continued to clear hanging clothes out of the closet, empty drawers and fold everything meticulously in her bags.

A pair of black Capri pants hung on a hook behind the bathroom door. Julie remembered that she'd slept in them the night she was outside the Solaria spa and dropped them in her dirty-laundry bag. She tossed her bathing suit and her avocado shorts in the laundry bag, too, depositing it in the hall outside the bathroom.

She turned to the closet door and was about to zip up the large garment bag hanging there that held their evening clothes, when something made her stop. *The Capri pants; I'd better check the pockets before I wash them. I think I left the sleeping pills in there.*

She rummaged through the bag and pulled out the pants. Sure enough, the pills were in her left pocket. *Wait. What's this?* There was a hard item at the bottom of the right-hand pocket. Julie fished it out. It was a distinctive pink and black Cartier pen.

Julie plopped on the couch, turning it under the lamplight: *Adrienne Paradis.*

Adrienne Paradis! How did Adrienne's pen come to be in her pocket? Julie was stumped; it was impossible! She'd hardly spoken to Adrienne that night. Certainly, she had never borrowed her pen. Suddenly, she remembered Alice Kent at the Captain's Table:

"Oh, Ms. O'Hara, I'm such a fan! I saw you on The View. Phil and I loved your seminar and we bought Clues, but we forgot to get you to sign it. I hope you don't mind; I brought it with me."

"Did you bring a pen?"

"Oh, yes," she said, waving the pen.

It happened all the time. Fans would present her with a copy of *Clues* and a pen to sign it. Julie recalled her pool-side conversation with Cathy Byrne:

"I understand Adrienne came back to the club?"

"Yes, she brought your book. She wanted you to sign it."

The Top Hat club was on Deck 12.

She was sleeping in front of the spa on Deck 12.

Julie sat back in shock.

I autographed Adrienne's book! She saw me there and brought it over to me. She gave me the pen to sign it, and walked off without it. Nothing else makes sense.

Julie forgot her packing and hurried over to Joe. She shook his shoulder.

"Joe, wake up. Wake up, honey."

"What? What is it?"

"I had Adrienne Paradis' engraved pen in my pants pocket."

Joe shook his head, trying to wake up, to understand what she was saying.

Julie gave him the pen. "This was in the pocket of the Capri pants I changed into the night Adrienne went missing! I was sleeping in front of the Solaria spa on

Deck 12. Adrienne had to have given me this *that night*, right before she was thrown overboard."

Joe got up, pulled on his briefs and stood silent, examining the pen.

"Do you remember her having a copy of my book?"

"Yes," he said, blinking. "She almost left it; she turned back and got it."

"I bet she saw me out there and brought the book to me. I must have signed it in my sleep. I don't remember it, but it's the only way I could have gotten her pen.

"Joe, I can't think of anything I do more automatically! I've signed hundreds of copies and I always date it and scribble the same thing: '*For Jane Doe, Best wishes, Julie O'Hara*'".

All at once, a scene played in her mind: Adrienne taken by surprise, airborne with her arms flailing…falling from a great height…headfirst into a dark, flickering sea.

The image was so frightening and real that Julie dropped to the couch and wrapped her arms around herself, shuddering.

It came to her at that moment.

Adrienne wouldn't hold on to a book. She would have dropped it immediately as soon as someone grabbed her.

"Adrienne went over, Joe. Not the book. She dropped it."

"So where is it?"

Julie looked up at him.

"Her killer has it."

46

How do you pack a dead woman's clothes? Dale gave up trying to fold Adrienne's things and just concentrated on filling her suitcases. He made sure that everything of hers was stuffed in her luggage, and then he put it all outside in the corridor. It would help not to be reminded of Adrienne's death.

If I could just get one good night's sleep without thinking about her...

The last few days had been hell. No one was treating him with compassion, as they should. Instead, there was an unspoken accusation behind every condolence. He couldn't wait to get off the ship, and yet he dreaded having to face Adrienne's sister, Marie, and their parents. They knew the state of his and Adrienne's marriage; they would be the *worst* to deal with.

Dale had come to the conclusion that he simply had to get on with his life, in spite of the cloud of suspicion that would probably dog him forever.

He heard someone rapping on his door.

Shit. Who the hell is that?

47

Three bags were set out in the corridor beside Dale Simpson's door. Julie whispered, "he must be here," while Joe knocked. A moment later, they heard him on the other side.

"Yeah? Who is it?"

"It's Joe Garrett, Dale."

Locks released. "Oh, hi. C'mon in," Dale said with a look of mild surprise. He looked better than he had of late, dressed decently in khaki pants, a shirt and a crewneck sweater.

Julie followed Joe in, a copy of her book, *Clues*, in hand. She saw the change in Dale right away. *Good, he hasn't been drinking.* "Hi, Dale…how're you doing?"

"I'm okay, Julie…thanks."

Joe couldn't help himself. There was just something likeable about Dale Simpson, and Joe was glad to see the guy cleaned up and sober. He put his hand on Dale's shoulder and smiled. "You're looking better, buddy."

"Thanks, Joe. Have a seat. Can I get you two something? I've sworn off the hard stuff, myself. Been overdoing it the last few days."

"No, thanks," Joe said. "Julie found something of Adrienne's she wanted to give you."

"Oh?"

"Yes," Julie said, handing him Adrienne's pen. "She gave me this to sign her copy of my book, see?" Julie opened the inside cover on a new copy where she'd just written:

June 18, 2012
For Adrienne Paradis
Best wishes,
Julie O'Hara

"I thought you'd want to have them," she said, handing him the book, all the while studying him carefully.

Dale appeared to be genuinely puzzled. He looked from Julie to the book, making no attempt to avert his gaze as one does when uncomfortable or guilty. He held the book and the pen in his left hand. His right hand was at his chin, positioned in the classic pose of Rodin's *Thinker*, with his index finger along his cheek and the other fingers curled under his mouth. His eyebrows were drawn together and he held the side of his lower lip between his teeth. Everything about him displayed his confusion.

"That's funny; she left these at the seminar?" He scratched his head. "I could have sworn she showed me your book right before we went to dinner. In fact, I *know* she did!" Dale stared at Julie now, his brow furrowed. "I sat right here and looked through it! How did you get these?"

Joe looked at Julie as if to say, *"I told you it wasn't him."*

"You're right, Dale," Julie said. "That's not her book. That's another copy, and I just autographed it ten minutes ago."

"I don't understand. This is her pen."

"I know. I'm sorry, but I had to test you with the book." She took it back from him and set it on the coffee table. "Come. Sit down. We've got some important information for you. I want to tell you how I came to have Adrienne's pen, and why my book is significant in all this."

Joe and Dale joined her around the coffee table.

"Monday, the eighteenth, the night of the Captain's Table dinner, Joe and I had a serious argument. Yes, some of it was sparked by Adrienne's behavior toward Joe, but mostly it was about Joe's drinking."

Joe cut in. "I go to AA, Dale. Didn't have a drink in years. Not until I got on this ship. Julie never saw me drunk before."

Julie nodded. "I over-reacted when Joe didn't want to leave the Top Hat. I went back to our stateroom alone, but I was so upset I didn't want to be there when he returned.

I tried to get another cabin, but nothing was available, so I changed into a pair of black Capri pants and went up to Deck 12, to the Solaria spa. I stretched out on a chaise up there and I took a sleeping pill…an Ambien."

"Ambien? That was risky," Dale said. "You could have got up and wandered around. I've heard of people doing that, even driving with no memory of it after taking those pills."

"Exactly. I'm glad you're familiar with that, because that's how I got Adrienne's pen. I just found it tonight in the pocket of the pants I was wearing. I'm convinced that we met up there, even though I have no memory of it. Here's what I think happened:

"First of all, you need to know that Adrienne left the Top Hat club and came back here to get her copy of *Clues*. According to Cathy Byrne, she wanted me to sign it. I think she knew I was mad at her for dancing and flirting with Joe. But, for whatever reason, she brought it back to the Top Hat. By that time, I was gone and so were you."

"Yes. I was mad at her, too. I went to the Casino."

"When the bartender was closing up, Adrienne told Joe she wanted to go for a walk on the deck," Julie said.

Joe nodded. "I wasn't interested in that; I wanted to find another bar."

"Anyway, Joe headed for the Promenade, and Adrienne went outside on Deck 12. When she got as far as the jogging trail, she must have seen me sleeping on the chaise in front of the spa; there was a recessed light directly over my head there. Although I don't remember it, I'm certain Adrienne brought the book over to me and gave me that pen to sign it with."

Dale was still confused. "I don't quite understand…"

"Dale, I'm sorry to say it, but I think Adrienne was stalked and attacked right after that. My point is that no one being thrown off a ship is going to hang on to a book. I think her copy fell on the deck."

"But they didn't mention finding any book. They don't even know where she went over."

"That's just it; I think the killer picked it up! Not only that, *I bet he still has it.* There was no time to decide whether to throw it overboard or not because of the spotlight camera panning fore and aft. Under pressure to do something or not do it, most people pick the safest choice…they do *nothing*. The killer had to duck to get out of sight, to make sure he didn't get caught on video. I think he grabbed the book and ran."

"For God's sake! Do you know who he is?"

"We think it was Gabe Rossi, the bartender who closed up the Top Hat that night. We just found out today that he has a history of rape and fooling around with female passengers. As an employee, he would have known about the cameras and where to hide to avoid them. We couldn't figure out any way to connect him to Adrienne, but if he's got her book…"

Dale jumped up and headed for the door. "That bastard's probably up there now!"

Joe grabbed him. "Wait, Dale! Rossi *is* working the

Top Hat tonight; we called to check. But we need to search his room and we've got no way to do it. We have to get Security involved here."

"Security? That's a laugh! It's a closed case, as far as they're concerned."

Julie put a calming hand on his arm. "I know. You're right. Clyde Williams isn't going to listen to us, particularly at this late hour. But I've got a plan." Julie pulled the Hotel Manager's card from her pocket. "Bob Sanchez knows about the problems with Rossi. In fact, Rossi doesn't know it, but he's getting fired tomorrow. I'm going to see if I can get Sanchez to convince Security to search his quarters tonight."

Dale spoke with controlled fury. "Call him. Now."

48

It was Friday, the last night of the cruise, and Gabe Rossi was having a very good night. Thanks to the crowd in the Top Hat club, his tip envelopes were piling up nicely. He was working the service bar, bantering with the waitresses as they queued up to get their drink orders. One of them, who wouldn't have been old enough to serve drinks in the US, had caught his eye. She was Gabe's type: tiny, dark-haired and playful. He felt himself getting hard. *I know what to do with a smart mouth like yours.* He smiled at her, flashing his beautiful white teeth and winked.

Behind the young girl, the heavy tempered-glass doors to the top-most deck were a barrier, separating all the music and gaiety inside the club from the wild wind and rain outside. If not for tropical storm Beryl, the service bar would be supplying drinks for passengers sitting at tables out there. Many of them would be relaxing by the railing, watching the Mystral's wake in the moonlight. As it was, flashes of lightning lit a bare expanse, a sheet of water rushing one way across the empty deck and then the other.

Gabe liked stormy weather. It was exciting and everyone partied like hell.

He'd have liked to see some of them go to hell, mostly men. Especially the rich ones like Gill Byrne. Women swooned around Byrne; he could have any one of them, anytime. *There's nothing special about him,* Gabe thought. *It's all about his money.* Bitches suck up to money and power. Like Adrienne Paradis, for example. Why else was she fucking an old married man like Byrne?

Gabe flexed the muscles in his broad shoulders, his biceps stretching the short white sleeves of his shirt. He unconsciously tightened his abs. *I could have shown Adrienne what a real power fuck was.*

Gabe had been setting up Adrienne Paradis for the last two cruises, reeling her in like a fish on a line. She was seeking him out, always showing up at whatever bar he was working, usually with the ballplayer in tow and the Byrnes. She didn't seem to care about her husband. *She got off on making Gill Byrne jealous, knowing he couldn't do anything about it.*

Gabe played the game because he got a kick out of that, too. But that last night should have been perfect. The Top Hat wasn't busy and he was closing up alone. Adrienne's eyelids were at half-mast; he could tell the drug was taking effect:

"Where are you going? I thought you were going to stay and have a drink with me."

"I need to go get a book. I'll be right back. Don't worry; I'll hang around."

Except Joe Garrett hung around, too, and fucked everything up.

It replayed in his head like a bad song that wouldn't die…

Monday nights usually sucked, but not as bad as this one. Gabe was all done cleaning up and he was getting madder and madder watching Adrienne hold hands with that drunken bum, Garrett. He went to the dimmer, turned the lights up full and tried to keep the anger out of his voice.

"That's it, folks…closing up now!"

Joe Garrett stood and pulled Adrienne up, too.

"C'mon, let's go find somewhere else to talk."

No, no! Gabe thought, as Garrett led her toward the etched glass double-doors, which stood open to the hall and the elevators.

Adrienne stopped and Gabe was relieved. "Wait a minute, Joe."

She returned to the table and Gabe smiled at her. Atta girl, he thought.

"I forgot my book," she said, waving it. "Good night, Gabe."

Good night? You bitch, Gabe thought. You BITCH!

He switched off the lights and hurried across the

club to lock the doors behind them. If he could have slammed them, he would have, but they closed slowly on their own. Garrett and Adrienne stood there in the hall at the elevators, oblivious, their backs to him. Gabe was furious; he stood there in the dark, his blood boiling, watching them through the etched glass.

"Shit, it's not working," said Garrett. "C'mon. Let's go down to the pub."

They took a few steps over to the stairs and Adrienne threw her arms around him and said, "Darling, I want to go for a walk outside. Come with me."

That BITCH!

"Nah. You go. I'm going downstairs."

Then she fucking kissed him goodnight...and Gabe decided to kill her.

Adrienne went out the starboard-side door at the end of the hall. A minute or two later, Gabe saw her come around and walk past the glass doors at the rear of the club. He ran to the doors and let himself out onto the deck hoping to trap her there, but she had already turned right and was walking up the port-side of the ship.

He walked fast, looking up, aware of the spotlight camera that hung from the bridge and panned fore and aft. Damn, it's turning back this way!

Suddenly, up ahead, Adrienne staggered off to the right. Good, he thought. She's out of camera range. I'll fuck the bitch first and then kill her! He cut in and saw her and then stopped cold, ducking into a dark corner.

He was beyond furious now. Who the hell is THAT?

While the spotlight panned the railing from the front of the ship to the back, an odd tableau played out in the shadows by the Solaria spa. Gabe watched as Adrienne shook and awakened Julie O'Hara, the body language expert. O'Hara scribbled something in Adrienne's book and immediately turned over and appeared to go back to sleep.

Adrienne stood there for a moment. Then she staggered back onto the jogging trail in the dark wake of the spotlight, panning back toward the front of the Mystral.

The BITCH was just standing there at the railing, asking for it!

Gabe rushed up and heaved her over the side.

The spotlight was headed back. What to do with her fucking book?

He grabbed it and ran.

"Gabe, Gabe? Hey! You got my martinis ready?" It was Adele, one of the older cocktail waitresses who'd been working in the Top Hat all week. Gabe hadn't realized it, but he'd actually stopped working and was staring out the glass doors.

"Oh, sorry, Adele. I'll have them for you in a minute. I was just checking out the storm." Gabe smiled and hustled to fill her drink order.

Stop thinking about it! It will show! Do you want to get caught?

Someone else killed Adrienne. Someone else...

49

The phone was ringing. Julie had it on "speaker" and Dale and Joe were listening, too.

"Officer Sanchez here."

"Officer Sanchez, this is Julie O'Hara."

There was a pause.

"Hello, Julie. What can I do for you?"

"May I call you Bob?"

"Of course. What can I help you with?"

Julie took a deep breath. "I know who killed Adrienne Paradis, Bob. And I believe I know how to prove it."

"What do you mean? You have an eye witness? Someone who saw Adrienne Paradis pushed overboard?"

"Well, no, not a witness."

"Then I'm afraid you can't prove that a crime was committed. I mean, without a body, these things are difficult to resolve, Julie. Unless someone saw something..."

"Well, I may not be able to prove that he killed her, but I believe I can prove that a man was with Adrienne out on Deck 12 right before she went overboard."

"It doesn't sound like you're talking about her husband, Dale Simpson."

"No, I'm not. In fact, Dale and Joe Garrett are listening to this call. I've got you on speaker."

Dale and Joe said hello, and the Hotel Manager acknowledged them.

"So, who are you accusing?"

"Someone on your staff ...Gabe Rossi."

"Gabe Rossi? The bartender?"

"Yes. The one who worked in the Top Hat the night Adrienne went missing. I've heard two rumors about him. One has it that Gabe has been known to mess around with female passengers; the other rumor is worse. I've heard about a woman, approximately the same diminutive size and coloring as Adrienne Paradis, whom he may have raped."

"Another passenger?"

"No, a young server. Listen, Bob. Let me tell you why I think Gabe Rossi killed Adrienne Paradis, and why I'm calling you, all right?"

Sanchez sighed audibly. "All right. Go ahead..."

One after the other, Julie sketched out the reasons why she and Joe had cleared the other diners who were in Adrienne's company at the Captain's Table the night of her disappearance. She didn't hold back, figuring that the "hotman" who ran everything probably already knew about Doctor Sinclair and Captain Collier, and Gill Byrne and his affair with Adrienne. As if to confirm that, there was nothing but silence on the other end of the line.

Julie continued and described the latter part of the evening in the Top Hat club, particularly Adrienne personally getting her own drink from Gabe Rossi...a drink that quite possibly contained a drug.

"Now, this is the part where you're going to have to bear with me, Bob..."

"I'm listening. Go ahead."

And then Julie told him about Adrienne going back to her room during the evening to get her copy of Julie's book so Julie could sign it. She told him how she had found Adrienne's designer pen this evening in the pocket of the Capri pants she had worn only once...the night she had slept outside on Deck 12.

"You're saying that you met with her there, and signed her book?"

"Not consciously, no. I took an Ambien sleeping pill and I don't remember anything. Nevertheless, I *do* think I signed her book. You see, people often hand me a pen for that purpose. Here's the point, Bob: I gave up trying to be original hundreds of copies ago. I always write the date and the same message: *For Jane Doe, Best wishes, Julie O'Hara.* I probably wrote that fifty times last Monday at my seminar. The odds are that I wrote that date and message in Adrienne's copy."

"Assuming that you did, what does it mean?"

"Nobody gets attacked and thrown off the twelfth deck of a ship hanging on to a book. I believe Adrienne dropped that signed and dated book, and I think Gabe

Rossi still has it…probably in his cabin. I'm calling to ask you to exert your influence to get security to search his quarters while he's at work tonight."

Julie shut up then. The three of them stayed quiet, waiting for the hotman's response, praying that he'd see it their way.

It seemed to take him forever, but finally he broke the silence.

"I can't do it, Julie. This is conjecture, speculation. And Gabe Rossi has a cabin mate, Matthew Graham, another bartender. We'd be invading Matt's privacy, as well as Gabe's. Look, I'm not unaware of the problems with Rossi. If it's any comfort to you, he's not going to be on any future cruises with Holiday Cruise Lines."

"It's no comfort to me or any other woman to know that a killer rapist is free."

Sanchez was silent…and Julie was wise enough to wait for him to speak.

"That's not fair, Julie. If we had an ounce of proof, we'd search his cabin."

"I have a way to get that proof! If you and Clyde Williams will back up Dale and Joe and me, I promise I can make Rossi think he's caught."

"You're proposing a sting?"

"Yes, and it'll work, Bob. What have you got to lose?"
More silence…

"All right. I'll call Clyde."

50

T hey came together at eleven o'clock and took the stairs to Deck 12. Silently, they crossed the hall and moved up against the wall opposite the elevators and next to the Top Hat's open doors. There were six of them, as Clyde Williams had brought Wes Hall for extra muscle. Clyde peeked around the corner and signaled that the club was empty except for Rossi.

According to their plan, Julie, apparently alone, would go in and confront him. She'd tell him she remembered signing Adrienne's book and had seen him that night. Julie's story would be that she had befriended the Head Housekeeper, Lana Medeiros, persuaded her to open up Gabe's cabin, and they'd found Adrienne's dated and autographed copy.

This will work, she thought. *It worked with Dale and it will work with Rossi. He'll make a move or say something. One way or another, his guilt will show and Clyde Williams will see it. I hope to hell Joe keeps Dale in check.*

217

Julie steeled herself and marched in with her newly autographed copy of *Clues*. Rossi was behind the service bar near the rear doors leading to the deck. If her plan was going to work, she needed to get him out of there, where they could rush him…if it came to that.

"Hello, Gabe."

Rossi was removing bottles from tiered shelves at the back of the bar and saw her in the mirror. "Well, hello," he said, turning and smiling. He was darkly handsome in a classic Italian way, with chiseled features and strong, white teeth. "Julie O'Hara, isn't it? You looking for your boyfriend? Mr. Garrett hasn't been in tonight."

"No, I'm not looking for Joe, he's asleep. I came here to show you something."

Julie stood in front of the deck doors, hoping Gabe would come out from behind the bar to see what she had in hand.

As agile as a panther, Gabe ducked under the bar. "So what is it?"

A flash of lightning behind the glass doors lit up one side of him, standing before her smiling like Sardonicus. The effect was frightening and Julie felt like running away but, all at once, a righteous anger began to flow through her, strengthening her. It was as if Adrienne was standing there without a voice, counting on her.

"It's Adrienne's book, Gabe, the one you hid in your cabin."

His smile gone, Gabe looked around, as if making sure they were alone.

"I don't know what you're talking about."

"I'm talking about *this*." Julie stepped forward and held the book open so he could see the date and the inscription. "Lana Medeiros let me into your cabin and I found it. I knew it was you I saw running off that night. You picked this book up off the deck right after you threw Adrienne Paradis overboard!"

Gabe looked around again and stared at her, his eyes hooded and calculating. "You're crazy. You didn't get that out of my room; I never saw that book before."

Julie took a gamble. "Don't be stupid, Gabe. It's over! You think I'd come here without insurance? I've got Malaya's crucifix, too."

Gabe's eyes flared, and in one swift move, he grabbed Julie and twisted her arm violently behind her back. She screamed as the pain ripped through her shoulder.

"YOU FUCKING BITCH! WHERE IS IT?"

Dale led the charge into the room. "LET HER GO, ROSSI!"

Suddenly, the heavy glass door behind them swung open and Julie fell backward. *Gabe was dragging her across the deck!* The wind howled and tore at them and they were instantly soaked by the heavy, blowing rain. Water washed over Julie's scrambling feet in cold, rushing waves. One of her flats came off and was immediately swept away in the near-total darkness.

The shouting men poured through the open doors after them, backlit by the light inside the club. Julie couldn't see Joe. *Where was he?* "JOE! JOE!"

"SHUT UP, BITCH! IF I'M GOING OVER, SO ARE YOU!"

He was shoving her up on the railing! She was hanging over from her waist, her feet off the deck, blinded by the rain, her wet hair whipping across her face. *Oh, God, help me! Please help me!*

Julie heard Joe yell, "NO!" as he slammed into Gabe from the side.

And then she fell, tumbling into the water.

51

"Follow me!" Bob Sanchez yelled to Joe as the two of them raced down the stairs to Deck 11. "We've got to pull her out fast!"

Joe had never been on this end of Deck 11. He saw immediately that the hallway there was a carbon-copy of Deck 12 above, the elevators facing a darkened club: The Crew Bar.

"This way!" Sanchez yelled as he held open the exterior starboard-side door against the wind and rain. They tore around the closed bar to its rear deck, where they heard Julie screaming into the pitch-black darkness.

"HELP! HELP ME!"

A bolt of lightning illuminated her being slammed, side-to-side, in the violently tossing sea-water pool reserved for the crew. "Don't get in!" the hotman yelled. "It's too dangerous! Grab her from the side! I'll get over there!" He ran to the port-side of the overflowing pool.

"JULIE! I'M HERE, BABY! OVER HERE!"

Julie turned and saw Joe's silhouette in the lightning. She reached out and swam hard against the wave, which was rushing to port. Joe leaned over and snagged her jersey, then grabbed her under her arms. "It's coming back, Julie…now!" As the high water hit the padded pool wall, he lifted her up and out, the two of them thrown back on the deck.

Bob Sanchez came running. "Is she okay? Are you okay, Julie?"

"I am now," Julie gasped, clinging to Joe.

"C'mon, we've got to get out of here," Bob said, as the two men helped Julie to her feet. They hung onto each other and whatever handholds they could grab; slipping and sliding, they made their way back to the starboard door. To their surprise, Michelle Sinclair was waiting there with two white-uniformed male nurses and a wheelchair.

"Clyde Williams called Captain Collier. They're all upstairs grilling Gabe Rossi," she said, moving the wheelchair forward and extending her hand. "Here, Julie. Sit down."

"Oh, I don't need a wheelchair! I'm fine; my shoulder's a little sore, that's all."

"Please, no arguments. We're going to get you down to the Medical Center and take a look. Come sit down, Julie."

"Go ahead, honey," Joe said, helping her into the chair. "I'll go to our cabin and bring you some clothes."

Suddenly, Julie didn't want to let go of his hand. "Promise you'll come right down?"

"Absolutely," he said, choking up. "I'll be right there."

Bob Sanchez smiled at Joe as the elevator doors closed on Julie, surrounded by her white-clad attendants.

"That's some woman you've got there, Joe."

"Damn straight."

52

A drienne was elated beyond measure...

She had loved Dale and now he would have peace. Because he had experienced a loss without compassion, Dale would be especially tender with her sister, Marie, and her elderly parents, Elise and Daniel. They would comfort each other and they would want him to continue his stewardship of their business. It would be a wise decision, and she knew they would be safe in his capable hands.

And Julie O'Hara! How she thanked God for her surrogate! Of course, He knew all along how everything would turn out. Her time with the Mystral had been a test...and she had passed.

"Adrienne" coalesced in joy, sparkling like a thousand stars...
Then she was gone.

53

It was two in the morning and Julie, sedated by a painkiller, was a little wobbly on her feet. She leaned heavily on Joe as he slipped his card key into 1272. He ushered her in and closed the door behind them.

"Omigod, Joe, look at this."

It was an enormous bouquet, mostly white roses.

"For you, babe, I'm sure."

Julie pulled out the card:

*"With the utmost gratitude for
your persistence and your bravery.
– Captain Andrew Collier."*

"Oh, isn't that nice, Joe?"

"Sweetheart, I think it's the least he can do. I'll be surprised if HCL doesn't make you a present of a free cruise. Can I help you get out of your things?" he said, pulling her sweater over her head.

"Joe. Stop treating me like an invalid. I'm okay!"

"That's not why I'm helping you undress…"

54

The next morning at eight, Julie and Joe were assigned to the Odyssey Lounge along with several others, including Dale Simpson and Gill and Cathy Byrne, who were all previously on Deck 10. They were to wait there until their group was called to disembark.

"Look at Dale," Joe whispered. "What a difference, huh?"

He's not the only one, thought Julie, checking out Gill and Cathy.

Their group number was called and Julie and Joe proceeded to the gangway on Deck 4.

After collecting their baggage in the terminal, they headed out to Joe's Land Rover for their hour-long drive back home. They were smiling, glad to be back in the Sunshine State.

"JULIE! JOE!"

It was Jon Reece, their British writer-friend, running after them, winded. "Could I possibly grab a ride with you into Orlando?"

"Of course," Joe said, taking his bags. "Hop in the back."

As they drove out of the parking lot, Jon Reece leaned forward and said, "I've decided to write a book. May I ask you a few questions along the way?"

"I can't see why not," Julie said. "Have you got a title?"

"I rather like 'Mystral Murder'…"

**Turn the Page
for A Preview of**

Topaz' Trap

**Julie O'hara Mystery Series
Book Four**

>>>

LEE HANSON

Topaz' Trap

A Julie O'Hara Novel

Book 4, Julie O'Hara Mystery Series

Topaz' Trap

PROLOGUE

Where is Topaz?

Dorothy Hopkins peeked through the Venetian blinds again, rubbing her swollen, arthritic knuckles. Her nine-thirty doctor's appointment weighed on her mind. If her neighbor didn't come soon, she'd miss it. The younger woman, thirty-eight, had taken on the responsibility of ferrying Dorothy, eighty-six, to her doctor's appointments.

It's not like Paz to be late, not like her at all.

Dorothy's fingers tingled as she fumbled with the phone and dialed her friend's number again. Topaz still didn't answer.

Maybe I should go over there. Perhaps she overslept.

All showered and perfumed in her lilac pantsuit and low-heeled Mary Janes, Dorothy decided to do just that. Tucking a few thin silver strands into her French twist, she picked up her black patent leather purse and put it over her arm. She patted Angel, her aging toy poodle. A warm sigh escaped her as she looked into her pet's adoring brown eyes.

"I'll be back in a little while, sweetheart. You have a nap."

Dorothy grabbed her wooden cane and went out her front door, double checking to make sure it locked behind her. She crossed the small courtyard to the sidewalk and glanced around, but no one was outside on their little cul-de-sac. She turned left, eyes on the ground, negotiating her way along the cement walkway, wary of a raised section between their townhomes that might cause her to trip. Having navigated the sidewalk, she pushed her glasses back up on the bridge of her nose, turned in and crossed her neighbor's courtyard. Hanging on to the wrought-iron handrail, she climbed two broad, shallow steps to a glossy black door with brass hardware.

Dorothy paused to catch her breath, and then she rang Topaz's bell and waited. No answer. Again she pushed the doorbell. She heard it ringing inside, but Paz didn't answer. At last, she tried the door. To her surprise, it opened, and she poked her head inside. A strange scent caused her to shudder, a fleeting frisson of fear.

"Paz? Are you home?"

Dorothy stepped inside, squinting and shielding her sensitive eyes from the blinding sun pouring in through tall, naked windows. She made her way through the dining area toward the kitchen, "Paz?"

Leaning on the cane, Dorothy forced her eyes open and gasped in shock as she found herself face-to-face with blood and horror on the kitchen floor, hideously spotlighted by the merciless glare of the sun. The cane clattered away along with her glasses as Dorothy collapsed, pressing her hands against her eyes to shield herself from the evil that filled the room.

Struggling for breath, she squeezed the Life Alert button hanging around her neck. She wanted to scream, *help me!*
But no sound came…

1

Julie O'Hara stepped into her condo and set her bag on a narrow glass-and-steel table under a frameless mirror. She dropped her keys into a mail basket with a couple of pencils and a roll of stamps and looked up. A late thirties woman bearing a resemblance to Julia Roberts frowned back at her in the mirror, her face a picture of guilt. Julie had just left her oversized Bengal cat, Sol, at the Eola Pet Hospital, where they would have to anesthetize him and put in some stitches... and it was all her fault.

The condo she shared with Sol was atop an elegant four-story building, nestled among sleek, taller ones, which overlooked Lake Eola, a twenty-three-acre urban jewel and its lovely park in Downtown Orlando. The morning's misadventure had occurred outside on her wraparound balcony.

Julie sighed in resignation. It was getting warm, and she twisted her heavy brown hair up in a knot, grabbing a pencil out of the basket and sticking it through to hold it. She turned, pulled a vacuum cleaner from the hall closet, plugged it in and ran it over the dark hardwood floor and across her treasured Oriental rug. The deep ruby and blue colors anchored the open room's décor, and Julie checked it carefully for tell-tale spots. Thankfully, there were none. Julie stashed the vacuum, grabbed a few disinfectant wipes and headed outside to clean up Sol's table.

Well, it wasn't really *his* table. Julie just thought of it that way because the big cat was always crouched there, watching the squirrels chase each other through the arms of the moss-draped oaks that surrounded the lake and stretched across Central Boulevard. Sol's comb and brush lay where she dropped them, along with her scissors… and little pink drops of blood.

Oh, God. How could I have done that to my baby?

Gone were all thoughts of what an ingrate and trouble-maker Sol was. Broken pottery and shredded trim on expensive throw-pillows were forgotten. Remorse had wiped his slate clean. It was an accident, of course. Julie was trimming a stubborn mat in Sol's fur under his back leg when he moved suddenly, and she clipped his skin instead. The cat so loved being groomed that he never ceased his deep, rumbling purr and didn't even seem to feel it.

Overcome with cat-parent guilt, Julie was slumped in a chair clutching her wipes and contemplating the crime scene when her phone rang. She stepped back inside to her desk—right-angled to a wall of books—and picked up.

"Hello?"

"Merlin, it's me. When are you coming in?"

Joe Garrett's tone and the use of her business moniker signaled something important.

"Why? What's up?"

"You know the Topaz Bonnefille case?"

"Is that the woman who was stabbed in Belmar last month?"

"That's the one. Listen, I've been hired to investigate it, Julie. I want to talk to you about it. Are you coming in?"

"Yeah, I had to take Sol to the vet, but I'll be in soon."

"Okay, see you. Bye."

"Bye."

Julie finished cleaning up outside. Miraculously, her creamy blouse was spotless, so she merely swapped her jeans and sneakers for a pair of tan slacks and flats, grabbed a sweater and left. She took the elevator down to the first-floor garage, walking past her VW convertible to the red Honda scooter tucked in front of it. Careful not to clip her neighbor's car, she backed the bike out. Once clear of the garage, she donned her helmet… and hit the pencil stuck in her makeshift bun. Smiling for the first time since her panicked run to the vet, she shook her hair out and slipped the helmet on.

Not exactly a Hell's Angel…

Julie hit the kickstand and hooked a right. She was headed for her office, just minutes away, around the other side of the lake. It was a perfect autumn day, a mix of mare's tail clouds and sun. All the trendy shops on Central Boulevard were doing a nice business. The lake was sparkling under the arms of century-old oaks, swan boats in the distance. A group of plein-air artists were sitting at their easels, capturing the lovely waterscape. Casual chatter and the aroma of food from sidewalk café tables reminded Julie that she hadn't eaten any breakfast, thanks to the morning's *cat*astrophe.

Soon, she was pulling into a bricked parking area in front of the large, vintage home that housed her office. The handsome two-story amber house angled toward the lake, its white columns gracing a wide veranda. Gold plates on the dark green double door were the only hint of its business use. The one on the right had only one word - *Merlin.*

Her book *Clues, A Guide to Body Language* had hit the best-seller list, and the single name was a godsend to all manner of promotions by her publisher. 'Merlin' was so busy doing guest spots on TV and working on the next book that she had to refer actual cases to other experts in her field. Intrinsically fascinated with unconscious communication and its forensic applications, success as a writer had been more of a side effect than a goal. Julie felt trapped in her work as an author, stuck in her office planning her itinerary or doing research on her computer.

She removed her helmet, looping the chin strap over her arm. *I haven't had an actual case to work on since the Mystral.* She remembered a cruise she and Joe Garrett had taken where a guest went overboard, and they were able to help solve the case. Shaking her head, she locked the scooter and climbed the front steps to the double door.

The gold plaque to her left announced *Garrett Investigations.*

Joe Garrett was more than Julie's landlord who occupied the other first-floor office. Over the last few years, he had become her colleague as a detective... and her lover... a fact they didn't even try to keep secret anymore. Julie unconsciously smiled as she thought of him.

Deciding to check in with Luz first, she turned right into her office. Her competent Latina assistant was busily typing at her desk. Twenty years Julie's senior, Luz was as tall as Julie, with heavy dark hair pulled back into a no-nonsense chignon. Julie had never seen her in anything but subdued clothing, something she suspected had to do with Luz' status as a widow. Somehow, just being in the office and seeing her substitute mom was helping Julie get over her guilt-trip.

"Hi!" Luz said, smiling. "I thought you were coming in earlier? You've got a couple calls on your desk."

"Yeah, I was. I had to take Sol to the vet." Julie quickly walked down the short hall to her office, keeping her transgressions to herself and forestalling further conversation on the subject.

Ignoring the familiar corner view of the park and its sparkling lake, Julie slid her helmet onto the file cabinet and sat down at her desk. She checked the calls and then proceeded to scan her email, answering a few and deleting a lot more. Caught up, she logged off, simultaneously checking her watch. It was a quarter past twelve already, and her stomach was grumbling.

She got up and headed back down the hallway.

"Luz, I'll call you later. I'm going over to see if Joe wants to go to lunch."

"Okay."

Julie hurried across the tiled foyer, past the central staircase that led up to Joe's apartment. Although he hadn't said, there was no way he would be upstairs this late in the day unless he was sick. *Which is never,* Julie thought with a smile, opening his office door.

Janet Hawkins, Joe's secretary, was seated on the immediate right at her desk, a neat affair with a family photo and violets. She was petite and curvy in a lime print dress, a sassy fifty-something with a short golden hairdo, courtesy of L'Oreal. "Good morning," she said, looking at her watch. "Oops, I guess it's afternoon!"

Julie smiled at her teasing. "Hi."

No doubt Janet and Luz had been chatting on the phone, wondering if she'd overslept. The two were best buds, romantics who gave themselves credit for bringing their bosses relationship to light. In a way, they were right. It's tough to keep a secret in a family, and the four of them *were* a family of sorts, working in Joe's inherited homestead, often on the same cases.

Across the open room, Joe looked up from his computer and grinned. He was dressed casually in a dark gray tee shirt and jeans. Ascribing to the idea that a cluttered desk was a sign of genius, every inch of his broad oak desk was strewn with papers and files. At six-four, with sun-streaked hair and a light beard, Joe was definitely a man to turn a woman's head.

"Hey, Merlin, you want to grab some lunch?"

"You read my mind. Want to go to Graffiti Junktion?"

Joe knew better than to suggest another restaurant at this moment. Julie was hooked on their signature Zucchini Fries, and apparently was contemplating a fix.

ALSO AVAILABLE
BY LEE HANSON:

Book 1, Julie O'Hara Mystery Series

CASTLE CAY

When her best friend is murdered, Julie O'Hara, a body language expert, packs up her suspicion and flies from Florida to Boston for his funeral. Who could have killed rising artist Marc Solomon, and what does Castle Cay, the Solomons' mysterious Caribbean island, have to do with it? Before long, Julie's sixth-sense pulls a hidden string that unravels a deadly conspiracy...and her own troubled past.

"A superbly-plotted murder mystery. In Castle Cay, Lee Hanson has meticulously crafted a fascinating murder mystery that will delight fans of the genre. Julie O'Hara is a complex, vibrant protagonist whose particular skill (she is a body language expert) is invaluable in helping her 'read' suspects. But it is when the reader learns about her tragic past that Julie really starts to jump off the page." *— Aman S. Anand*

"Page-turning suspense novel. Author, Lee Hanson, does an excellent job of building suspense in this murder mystery. She writes likeable characters who are well developed, adding interest to the plot. I see that there is a second book available, Swan Song. I would definitely be interested in reading further books in this series..." *— Dr. Beth Cholette*

"Loved this book! Lee Hanson has burst upon the scene with a can't-put-it-down, great new read. The author manages to weave a plot that is both intriguing and original. She leaves the reader with an unexpected, subtle twist at the end..."   – *Veritas*

LEE HANSON

Swan Song

A Julie O'Hara Novel

Book 2, Julie O'Hara Mystery Series

Swan Song

As dawn breaks, the pale body of a beautiful, raven-haired young woman is discovered in an errant swan boat, adrift on a small lake, smack in the middle of a jewel-like park in Downtown Orlando. It looks like a suicide, Snow White in a fractured fairytale. Body language expert, Julie O'Hara, isn't buying it. And that's a BIG problem, since Julie is the one person most likely to figure it out.

"Engaging and Unique. This is the second book in the Julie O'Hara series, coming after Castle Cay, and to say that I was impressed is an understatement. This novel had me hooked right from the start and the idea behind Julie and her career is a unique one. In my opinion, this was a very fresh and clever way to leap into the mystery/suspense genre. This was plotted very tightly...it took me by surprise when the true assailant was finally uncovered." — *Dianne E. Socci-Tetro "Books & Chat"*

"Twists and turns that keep you on your toes! A page-turner that will have you guessing till the very end. Normally, I'm pretty good at calling the villain in a whodunnit but in this case I was quite surprised. Like the movie "Sixth Sense", I wanted to go back immediately to see all the clues that I missed." — *Grace Martin*

"Another winner! Swan Song, the second book in this series, is perhaps even better than the first, Castle Cay. The plot has many intricate twists and turns without becoming confusing, and the characters are complex and appealing. Julie's relationship with Joe is a compelling subplot. Her special talent as a body language expert is quite believable. Over all, an excellent mystery." *– AK Mystery Mom*

Lee Hanson, a Boston native and Florida transplant, is the author of The Julie O'Hara Mystery Series, including *Castle Cay, Swan Song, Mystral Murder* and *Topaz' Trap*. Her novels, featuring body language expert, Julie O'Hara, have been called "the answer to a mystery addict's prayer," a line that makes the author smile… and keeps her writing.

Printed in Great Britain
by Amazon